THE SLUTTY HOTWIFE

5 MFM Wife Sharing Stories

MAKING ME A SLUTTY WIFE
THE SLUTTY WIFE'S VACATION
SLUTTY WIFE UNLEASHED
SLUTTY WIFE ON EDGE
THE SLUTTY WIFE'S DESIRES

LACEY CROSS

CONTENTS

ABOUT

This curious wife leaves no stone—or enticing entry—unturned.

When my husband reveals his deepest fantasy—to share me with other men—I'm reluctant at first. But once I get a taste of freedom, there's no going back. What starts with a steamy encounter at the veterinarian's clinic spirals into a daring journey of ever-bolder adventures.

From naughty vacations to sensual dances, I explore the intoxicating world of a hotwife—all with my husband's enthusiastic encouragement. The more men desire me, the more empowered and insatiable I become.
But with each scorching encounter, one question burns hotter: will my husband finally indulge my ultimate fantasy and share every part of me... or will he keep me on the edge, always craving more?

Dive into this five-book collection that follows hotwife Erin's journey from curious wife to unleashed.

To my amazing readers,

This series wouldn't exist without your incredible support and enthusiasm. When I wrote the first book to help pay for my cat's unexpected vet bill, I never imagined it would turn into such a wild and wonderful journey.

Your love for Erin, Ian, Jace, and Matt inspired me to continue exploring their story, and I'm so grateful for your encouragement every step of the way.

This might be the last books with them, but there are many more wife sharing adventures to write!

Love,

Lacey

P.S. My real cat, Buddy, sends his purrs and appreciation, too!

Making Me a Slutty Wife

Hotwife Exploration 1

Lacey Cross

Chapter 1

As I stroll into the vet clinic on Friday afternoon to pick up my cat, I think about my husband Ian's offer to open our marriage and allow me to fuck other men. For the last couple of months, we've been discussing the idea of me being a hotwife, and I've been hesitant. I don't need other men. Sure, the idea sounds appealing, but it's not worth risking my marriage over—at least, I didn't think so, but after a deep conversation last night, Ian made it clear that this is something he wants to try if I'm willing.

I find it hard to believe he wants me to fuck other people and then tell him about it, and that he doesn't want to go out and find himself a side piece as well. But he asked me to look up a bunch of stuff on the internet about hotwives, and I guess it's a legit thing.

Last night, after admitting that the idea turns me on, I finally agreed to it. Fucking other men with his permission sounds great, but I don't know how I'm going to find someone I actually want to do this with. Ian left it up to me to decide when and with whom for the first time. He wants it to feel right for me. But what if it never feels right? That's the problem.

The veterinarian clinic is deserted. It's a new clinic and I've never been here before. Buddy, my old-man cat, had a chipped tooth, and they needed to put him under to pull it. They wanted to keep him overnight to monitor him, so my husband dropped Buddy off yesterday and prepaid. All I have to do is grab my kitty and head out.

I sit down on a chair and wait for someone to notice I'm here. The pressure of the bench against my pussy reminds me I've been turned on all morning. I might have to go home and do something about it. After the talk with Ian last night, I had a sex dream where I was getting railed by a bunch of men in an alley. Not really what I'm into, but I guess my brain liked the idea in a dreamland.

Finally, the front desk worker pops out from the back room. She's a young, pretty woman with black hair and she greets me. "Oh hey, sorry. I didn't hear you come in."

Her friendly smile sets me at ease. "Oh, it's fine," I respond, as I return her smile.

She gestures toward the clinic area. "Come on back. We're closing early today and you're our last appointment. The vet wants to go over some things with you," she offers sweetly.

I follow her into an exam room. Since the office is new, everything sparkles and is spotless. The examination table is a long, brushed metal surface at waist height. The room is fairly bare other than a counter, and a bench against the wall, but that probably makes it easier to clean.

The front desk woman checks my cat's file. "Okay, wait here and I'll let Jace know you're ready."

I thank her and settle in on the bench. Pulling out my phone, I text my best friend, Sasha, to continue the conversation I had this morning with her about Ian's desire for me to fuck other men. We had to stop mid conversation so I could come and get Buddy. It looks like she messaged me while I was driving here.

Sasha

> Wait, did you take your cat to the new vet place on the corner of 64th?

What's this? This place has a reputation? I hope she's still on her phone, and I quickly reply.

Yeah, is something wrong with this place?

When I see chat bubbles pop up showing she's typing, I relax. Okay, she'll give me the dirt.

Not wrong... but that's the place with the super hot vet who gives "extra" services to women if they ask for them.

Um... what the fuck is she talking about?

Extra services. Like clip the cat's nails if I ask?

She replies with a big laughing emoji.

You're so naïve, it's adorable. No, if someone asks for extra services and makes it obvious they want sex, he'll fuck them.

I actually laugh out loud at that. It's so messed up. But there's no way I'm paying some dude to fuck me. It doesn't matter how hot he is. Huh, who knew we had a gigolo vet in town? Go us.

I'm NOT interested, but did anyone say how much he charges?

She sends me another laughing emoji.

It's free. If you want to fuck him, just tell him you heard about extra services and are interested in what he offers. Your husband said you could fuck someone else, so why not?

Oh God, she's crazy. I'm about to tell her so, but the exam room door opens, and I quickly set my phone down. My mouth drops open as the vet walks in.

Holy shit.

He's probably in his late thirties, and he's smoking hot. His dark brown hair is swept back, accentuating the deep blue of his eyes. His lab coat is unbuttoned over a pair of blue scrubs, which doesn't hide his powerful, fit frame.

I immediately can tell he's a dominant guy. He commands the room with his sheer presence, and I imagine being on my knees for him. Yep, I'm totally a thirsty slut.

"Hi, I'm Jace." He holds out his hand and I stand up to shake it. As my palm touches his, a tingle of desire ripples down my spine. Mmm, yeah, I'd take extra services from this guy, but no way would I ask for them.

"Hey, I'm Erin." My voice sounds breathy, but I can't help myself.

He shoots me a sexy grin. "Nice to meet you."

I try to hide how immediately attracted I am to him, and give him a soft smile. "Nice to meet you too."

Jace is taller than I am, and I imagine him bending me over the exam table. This is what I get for having a sex dream and not getting myself off this morning. I should have been playing with my toys instead of watching reality TV shows and chatting with Sasha until I had to come pick up Buddy.

Jace spends a few minutes going over how Buddy is doing and has a list of instructions for after-surgery care. He said it's all on the form, so once I know Buddy will be okay, I barely pay attention. I'm too busy looking at his thick fingers holding the paper and daydreaming about him dominating me.

I don't even know where the thought is coming from, but something about him exudes confidence and control. A desire to surrender overtakes me as my pussy pulses and I feel my panties grow wet. Yeah, I'm totally going to play with my toys when I get home and imagine this guy fucking me.

He's staring into my eyes deeply as he talks, and I can feel my pulse race as my body responds. The corners of his mouth lift and his eyes twinkle, as if he can tell what I'm thinking.

I'm suddenly unsure of what to do with my hands, and I rub them against my jeans self-consciously. I want to lick every inch of his gorgeous body, and then ride his cock like I'm on the Tilt-A-Whirl at the fair.

When a tap on the door interrupts us, it opens and reveals the front desk worker as she pops her head in. "Hey, is it okay if I head home? Everything is locked up."

"Sure, have a good weekend." Jace gives her that sexy smile of his and she blushes—yeah, I don't blame her.

She closes the door behind her and it's just me and Jace in the exam room again. Alone. My heart hammers as his eyes land on mine and electricity sizzles between us. Um, wow... I can tell he finds me attractive, but he's probably got all the neighborhood women drooling and hoping to fuck him. Hell, who knows how many people were in here already today asking for extra services. He might be exhausted.

There's no way in heck I'm going to fuck the vet—that just doesn't happen outside of books and movies—but I could flirt with him a little just to see what he says. I keep my voice silky smooth. "Does your office offer any extra services?"

The hot vet grins and he rakes his eyes over my body, making my nipples harden. Oh yeah, he didn't misinterpret my meaning. I wish he would rip my clothes off right here. His eyes burn with intensity. "Not if you're married. It's bad for business if an angry husband comes storming in."

He looks down pointedly at the wedding ring on my hand, and I almost laugh. Holy shit, Sasha was right. He DOES fuck women who come in. God, why is this idea so hot? Do I just want to be a number? It's a good thing I'm not seriously considering doing this... I don't think.

There's a noticeable bulge in his scrubs. Oooh, he's turned on. Shame and desire burns in my throat, and my brain blips out. All I can think about is fucking him, and I feel like such a slut.

I didn't expect to get so turned on by the temptation of fucking someone other than my husband. Talking about it was just theoretical, but being here with the possibility of it actually happening makes my pulse quicken with forbidden longing.

I fight the urge to sway towards him as a lusty feeling of warmth settles over me. Hell, why don't I fuck him? My husband wants me to. I can text Ian afterwards and tell him to come home prepared to hear about my slutty adventure.

Wet heat flares between my legs, and my body lights up as I make my decision. I'm going for it. It's time to make it clear what I want.

I keep my eyes glued to his as I run my fingers up his forearms and give him a coy smile. "I am married, but I have permission to play."

The corners of his mouth quirk as he moves closer and reaches out to finger a lock of my dark hair. I let out my breath and lower my eyes at his touch. "So your husband is fine with you fucking other men?"

He caresses my cheek, tracing along my jawline until he reaches my chin and tips it up so I'm gazing into his eyes again.

I hold my breath. The thought of fucking Jace makes me hotter than I can stand. I'm dying for him to press his lips to mine.

His words are like velvet. "Because I have to warn you, I'm not gentle and I like to share."

Um... share? The question must be in my eyes because he answers me. "You've got a beautiful mouth. I'd love to see your lips wrapped around my technician's cock while I fuck you."

Ooooohhh... My pussy flutters, and a wild impulse rises within me. This is something I haven't done before. The idea of strangers sharing me makes my inner muscles clench. My husband didn't say I could fuck two guys, but he didn't say I couldn't either. Does one more cock matter that much?

I take a breath and gather my courage.

I answer him honestly. "I'd like that." My heart races and I continue without thinking. "I want to feel your cock inside me."

His hand slips around my neck, and I lean towards him. I'm about to throw all caution to the wind and let this sexy stranger do whatever he wants to me.

The door to the room opens, interrupting us. I jump back from Jace when a guy in his twenties enters. He's got scrubs on and has a name tag, so he must be the technician whom Jace wants to see in my mouth.

The new guy smiles. "Hey, I'm Matt."

Hot damn. He's freaking gorgeous. Matt has short, blonde hair and deep-set, gray eyes. But the part that makes me warm and tingly is that his arms are covered with tattoos.

I never thought a tattooed man would do it for me, but Matt is hot. He's an Adonis of masculinity that makes my entire body ache. I love how he exudes a raw, sexy, male energy. He's definitely my type of guy, and he's definitely too young for me in any other circumstance but this.

Mmm, both of them together at once? Yep, I want this. I let out a breath and I try to compose myself. I'm acting like a wanton slut, but I can't help it.

Jace nods towards me and speaks to Matt. "Erin would like some additional services. Are you interested in joining us?"

Matt looks up and down my body, and his eyes take on a gleam. "Oh, yeah."

Shit, they do this together often? I mean, looking at them, I'm not surprised. This makes it even dirtier.

"Matt, why don't you go make sure Buddy is comfortable, and then come back so we can help Erin."

Matt grins at me and leaves. When the door closes, Jace turns to me and raises a questioning eyebrow. "I need to hear you say it. Say you want to fuck us both."

I didn't expect the need for explicit consent, and my mind whirls. My college years weren't crazy, so this is the sluttiest thing I've ever done in my entire life. I don't know if Ian is ever going to want me to do this again, so I better make this good. Go big or go home, right?

My brain buzzes as I imagine being their shared fucktoy. There's no question that I want this, but it's more than just fucking someone. There's something that my sweet husband can't give me and I think Jace can: I crave roughness. I want to be boneless with pleasure and sore when they're done with me, and go home feeling used. I want to be the ultimate slut who lets strangers fuck her and leave her dripping with their cum.

Oh, he's waiting for my answer. I lower my eyes again and my voice is soft. "Yes, please fuck me. Use me however you want to use me." Oh god, I feel a hint of shame for being such a slut, but I push it aside and add firmly, "You can do whatever you want to my mouth and my pussy. I want you both to take turns fucking me and filling my holes."

I peek up at him and his lips curl as if he's pleased and his gaze glitters with undisguised lust. "Good girl."

His 'good girl' sizzles my brain and the air becomes charged with sexual energy. Ohhhh, I think he's going to give me what I want.

He hooks his fingers into the waistband of my jeans and pulls me towards him. "It's time for you to undress so I can examine all your holes."

The next thing I know, he releases the button of my jeans and he's bending me over the side of the examination table. Since the table is too high for my feet to reach the floor, he has to boost me up. The surface is slippery and I grab the edge to hold on. I kick my sandals off while he pulls my jeans down, exposing my blue cotton panties. I would have worn something sexier if I had known this was going to happen, but he doesn't seem to care.

"What a good little slut." He rubs my pussy through my panties and my head spins. I love the harsh, dirty talk. He can call me whatever he wants.

As he peels my jeans all the way off, I study a chart on the wall that shows how to tell if your cat is obese. Yep, Buddy is a chonky boy. This entire moment feels surreal. Today was just a normal day. How did I get here?

He slips a finger under the band of my panties, seeking my clit. A pulse of joy in my core makes me gasp. Yeah, who cares how I got here? This is fabulous. If they spit-roast me, it's going to fulfill a fantasy I've dreamed about but never thought would happen.

I listen to the sound of his zipper going down while he continues to rub circles around my clit. Soft pings of delight radiate through me. Ohhh... this is definitely happening. He moves my panties aside and pulls my hips up, spreading my legs apart with his. When I feel the head of his cock probing my slit, I don't dare to breathe, afraid I might accidentally wake up if this is a dream.

The pressure against my entrance increases, and then with one fierce thrust he buries himself to the hilt. My mouth falls open as I give a long moan from the intense bliss. My fingers grasp the side of the table tighter as he fills me. Fuck... this feels so good. I want more.

I peep out tiny cries, and try to push backwards against him. He digs his hands into my hips roughly and forces me to hold still. He lets out a harsh growl. "Let's get one thing clear, little slut. I'm in control." His hand moves to my lower back, and he shoves me flat against the cool surface.

I whimper and pant as I obey his command to lie still. I want more, so much more. His hands move from my hips to cup my ass and squeeze it tight before he plunges back inside me with one deep thrust. "Fuuuuck," I cry out as my hands clutch at the sides of the exam table. His thrusts become powerful and rapid. Each slam into me jars me forward. I struggle to remain in the same position, so he won't stop again.

"I think I found a pussy that needs testing," he mutters darkly as he plunges in and out of my slick folds. His words send shivers of delight through me. He can test that hole all he wants.

Suddenly, he withdraws, and I yelp at the unexpected loss. I'm addicted to his length already. An unfamiliar madness seizes me and I writhe and mewl out in protest. I need more—more of him, and I need to suck on Matt.

His voice brings me back from my fantasies. "Did I say you could move?" he scolds. I freeze, my body shaking as I fight an impulse to look at him over my shoulder. I need to remember this is his show. Biting my lip, I shake my head in response and whisper, "No."

His hands slowly trace the curve of my ass before moving between my legs again. I lift my hips without thinking, offering my dripping sex to him, and he rewards my efforts with two fingers delving into my tight channel. My juices drip over his fingers, and my breath hitches as he finger fucks me while spanking my ass.

Shit... fuck... I wasn't expecting him to spank me. He's not doing it hard, but a fuzziness steals over me and I can feel myself sinking further into the mindset of being just a fucktoy. This is what I wanted, and it's glorious.

I struggle to obey his command to not move. Each thrust of his fingers creates an inferno of need inside me. I'm moaning, and start mindlessly grinding against his hand and lifting my ass with every spank.

When he pulls his fingers out of my pussy and I feel him rubbing my asshole with them, I cry out. Oh god, what is he doing?

He wraps my hair around his fist and pulls my head back. "Stay still, you filthy slut. I said I had to examine you."

I squirm on the table as he continues to massage my forbidden hole. Fuck, this is so hot, and I'm loving the new level of depravity I'm willing to allow. I want to feel him inside my ass so much, and I've never had anal sex. If he goes for it, I won't stop him.

A whimper escapes me as he releases my head and grasps my hips. I inhale sharply, trembling as I await his next move. He forces my legs farther apart and I hold my breath. Is he going to do it? His hands spread my ass cheeks, and the tip of his cock nudges my asshole.

Oh god. It feels good. Tension coils low in my belly as the pressure increases and I expect him to slip inside at any moment, but he backs off.

His voice is low and strained. "We'll leave that hole for your next visit."

His words sizzle my brain, and I whimper when he plunges his cock back into my pussy. Ohhhhh, fuck. This is more intense than before. He feels so big. He stills and caresses my ass. I start to pant and let out a long exhale. God, it feels amazing. My pussy pulses in excitement and the rapture builds in layers.

I'm so far gone, I almost don't hear the door open until Jace laughs. "Took you long enough. Erin's been begging to suck someone's cock."

"Oh, yeah?" Matt's voice sounds amused, and I want to protest that I really wasn't begging to suck on anything, but I stay quiet. Whether or not I voiced it, I do want to suck on him. I want everything. If Jace had shoved his cock in my ass, I would have thanked him and asked for more.

Jace holds my hips firmly, and my body vibrates with intense pleasure as he pounds into me relentlessly. His rhythm drives me closer and closer to the brink of ecstasy. I can feel my orgasm about to peak, and I rock my hips back against him, encouraging him to increase the pace.

Instead of going faster, he pulls out and slaps my ass. "Get on all fours. It's time to see those pretty lips wrapped around his cock."

Mmmm, yes. I scramble down on the floor and close my eyes as Jace kneels behind me. The cold tiles bite into my knees, but I don't care.

"Be a good slut and let Matt use your mouth," Jace commands as his fingers brush against my clit.

"Yes, I'm a good girl," I murmur as Matt kneels in front of me and pushes the spongy head of his cock against my lips. I open my mouth eagerly, and he guides his shaft in. He tastes different from my husband, but it's not unpleasant. His cock is thick, and I swirl my tongue along the veins, enjoying his groan of pleasure.

Nothing matters at this moment other than both of them filling me. I'm a slut who wants to get used by whoever wants me. If there were more men in the room, I'd beg them all to fuck me. This is the dirtiest thing I've ever done in my life. I can't believe I'm being so shameless. I really am a slut.

I moan around Matt's thick shaft as Jace plunges into me again, and my body shakes with desire as my pussy spasms. This is beyond messed up, and I love it. My moans grow louder as both men ravage my mouth and my pussy. The tension builds quickly this time, and soon I'm close to tipping over the edge again. My thighs tense and my toes curl as I inch closer to my orgasm.

Matt and Jace fuck me harder as I moan and try to match their pace. I lose myself in the bliss of their cocks driving into me, sucking harder as Matt pumps in and out of my mouth.

"Mmm, mmmm..." I groan loudly around him, struggling to take every inch of his cock. Matt responds with a loud grunt, "Oh, fuck. That's it, baby."

It feels so good and I bob up and down, swallowing him all the way until he hits the back of my throat. I choke, but don't stop. I need to satisfy them both, and I force my throat to relax so Matt can slide in and out easier. Whenever Jace whacks against my ass, it forces Matt further into my mouth. They're fucking both my holes at an unrelenting pace. This is so wonderfully dirty.

It's not long before I lose all semblance of control. My legs tremble as Matt and Jace work in tandem, alternately plunging into my mouth and my pussy. The ecstasy builds until I can't take it anymore. I explode, and a loud moan escapes my mouth as waves of rapture crash into me. My pussy quivers around Jace's cock as the bliss continues to spike.

Neither man stops pounding into me, even as I melt underneath them. When Matt shoots his cum down my throat, I drink every drop. "Mmm, yes, good girl. Swallow every bit," he says huskily.

I savor the flavor of his essence on my tongue and revel in the feeling of being used. Who knew I would like this so much?

Jace picks up speed behind me, and his harsh breathing tells me he's close. He's grunting in pleasure as his thrusts become faster, and soon his groans of ecstasy echo through the room as he empties his hot seed inside me.

"Ah, fuck," he sighs before pulling out. A rush of his cum mixed with my juices splashes on my leg and it shocks me back to my senses. I'm on my knees in the middle of the exam room with two guys I just met, and all I want is more.

I lean forward and rest my head on my arms, whispering hoarsely, "Wow."

Both men laugh in appreciation.

The men talk briefly while I float in a daze of joy. Matt leaves the room to check on my kitty, and Jace cleans me up with some wipes and helps me dress. When I'm ready, I stand there staring at him awkwardly. How does he end these encounters with other women? Does he wish them a happy life? I can't think of what to say, and I'm relieved when Jace speaks first.

"Erin, that was wonderful. Are you all right?"

He brushes away a strand of hair that is sticking to the side of my face and tucks it behind my ear. I can only nod yes. My head is spinning and my legs tremble, but I feel incredible. My body feels deliciously used, and my mind is mush. I've had plenty of great sex, but this experience is easily in the top five. It's not even that I took two men at once, though that was incredible. It was the depravity of letting my vet fuck me in his office and use me like a toy while sucking on another worker that made it a mind-blowing experience.

Shit, I hope Ian still lets me fuck other people. I don't want this to be a one-time thing. I want to be a hotwife now.

He puts his hands on my shoulders and gazes down into my eyes. "Are you okay with driving home?"

This time I can find my voice and do more than just nod. "Yeah, I'll be fine. Just a little overwhelmed."

He gives me a gentle kiss on my lips. "It's not always like this. You're a very special person."

I can't help the rush of joy I get from his words. Even if he says that to all the women, it's still nice to hear.

He pulls out his cell phone. "Can I have your number so we can talk later?"

It doesn't cross my mind to say no. "Yeah, sure." I rattle off my cell phone number and he punches it into his contact list.

"Thanks." He winks at me. "It's always fun to get to know someone outside of a one-night stand."

I don't know why since I just fucked him, but I feel shy. This entire experience has been intense, but in a good way. He runs a hand through my hair tenderly, and it surprises me when it feels so natural.

I want this to continue, whatever this is.

He touches his forehead to mine, and we stay that way for several moments before he steps back and walks me out to the lobby. Matt is waiting with my cat in the carrier, and I wave goodbye to the guys on my way out.

On the drive home, I hum to the music on the radio, thinking about how crazy this day has been. I can't wait to tell my husband all about it, and hopefully he wants me to continue being a hotwife. Hell, I just gave my number to the vet, so maybe someday I'll fuck him again.

This hotwife thing could work out nicely after all.

CHAPTER 2

I almost call Ian while I'm in the car, but I figure it's better to wait until I can focus on the conversation. I hope he doesn't get mad that I took on two men. It's not like they were both in my pussy, so it'll be fine, right?

He gave me permission to fuck other guys if it felt right. And this definitely felt right. Two hot, well-hung men devoured me. I love how they fucked me until I was almost mindless with lust. I need more of that in my life.

After I get home and make sure Buddy is fine, I sit down in the living room with a bottle of water and a snack so I can text my husband. When I woke up this morning the day seemed so ordinary, and now I feel as if my life has completely changed.

My hands shake with excitement as I type.

Erin

> Something crazy happened today. Do you want the details now, or later?

Ian

> I'm stuck on a stupid Zoom meeting and it's boring. Tell me now.

Okay! Remember your request from last night? About fucking another guy? Well, one just kind of fell into my lap today. It was the vet, and he invited a co-worker to join in. So I got to play with them BOTH! I guess I'm a hotwife now. I really hope that's what you want to hear, because I loved it.

My fingers hover over the screen, not sure how much more I should write. It takes forever for him to respond, and when he does, I giggle.

Fuck, I have a tent in my pants. Did they come inside you?

Mmm, oh yeah, they filled me so much it was running out of me.

They sure did.

Was it just your pussy or did they fill other holes?

Um... holy shit, Ian is totally into this.

My pussy and my mouth.

Which did you enjoy more?

A delicious naughty feeling shoots through my body as I think about the two men. It's hard to compare because they didn't both fuck me, but Jace is closer to my age and I loved his dirty talk. I don't want my husband to feel threatened, so I try to be cheeky.

I prefer your cock.

Hah, tell the truth.

I can't lie, but I can change the subject.

This is silly. You have a hotwife now, who you can play with as often as you want. Come home so I can fuck you.

I feel bad for him if he has a raging erection. Poor baby is going to just have to wait until he gets home. I look and it's barely 3pm. Shit, he won't be home for a couple of hours. This is going to be torture for me as well.

You're changing the subject, but fine, I'll wait for the details. I want you naked in bed when I get home.

It's a date.

I rub my nipples through my shirt and pull at the stiff peaks. I need Ian's mouth on my breasts tonight. The girls didn't get much attention today, and I'm feeling needy. I'm tempted to touch myself and use a toy, but I want to wait for Ian. Tonight is going to be fun.

Oh shit, I better tell Sasha what happened. That will entertain me for a bit. She'll be amazed at my sluttiness. I type away on my phone with glee and get lost in conversation with her.

I'm naked in bed with my eyes closed when Ian gets home. I'm playing with my tits and have a vibrator pushed into my wetness while I daydream about my slutty vet appointment.

My eyes snap open when he walks through the door. I shoot him a lusty smile and remove the vibrator so he can see the moisture coating my fingers. "Welcome home, honey. Would you like a taste?"

He takes a step towards me, but instead of diving for me as I hoped, he strips off his clothing slowly. I lick my lips when I see his cock. It's standing straight out, hard, and glistening with his pre-cum. When he sits on the bed, he growls, "No, you're going to come up here and straddle my lap so you can ride my cock while you tell me about what you did with the vet and his employee."

A delicious shiver races through me. When did he get so bossy? I like this version of him. I climb into his lap and guide his hardness to my pussy, moaning from delight as he fills me. My body tenses for a second and then relaxes as I adjust to him. He likes it when I'm on top.

"Okay, I'm not sure where to start."

His mouth lands on mine, and I lean forward and wrap my arms around his neck as I rock against him. He tastes spicy and warm—like I'm home. My pussy contracts around him and his hands wander to my tits. He pulls a breast to his mouth and sucks. His touch is so familiar, and I moan, "God, this feels so good. You know just what I like."

When he flicks his tongue around my nipple and sucks harder, I moan louder and grind on the base of his cock. This is why sex with my husband is always going to be better than with anyone else. He knows exactly how to give me the most pleasure. After so many years together, we're like a well-oiled machine, and the experience today highlights that. Fucking other men was fun, and was an amazing experience, but coming home to Ian is what makes it awesome.

As I bounce up and down on my husband's thick shaft, I share the details of my crazy day. I tell him about what Sasha told me, and how I propositioned the vet. I explained what they both looked like, and paint a vivid picture of how they fucked me. Telling Ian about my slutty exploits is erotic, and I slam down harder on him with each new admission.

Once I think I'm done with the story, I'm about to fuck him furiously and try to get him to blow his load, but I realize I left something out.

"Oh, honey..."

He rolls us over on the bed so he's on top and feasts on a breast before answering. "Yes?"

A spiral of desire makes me arch against him, and I'm breathless when I speak. "I forgot to mention something."

"Mmm hmm?" He switches breasts and sucks on my other nipple harder than usual.

I squeal from the pleasurable pain and buck against him, forcing his cock in as deep as he can go. Fuuuck, he's driving me insane.

He tugs on my nipple with his lips and murmurs, "Tell me."

Fuck! Okay. "Jace didn't fuck my ass, but he fingered it."

Ian stops all movement and looks up at me. "You let him stick his finger in your ass?"

Oh, shit... is he pissed? I open my mouth to tell him he didn't actually stick his finger in, but I don't have time to think because Ian sits back on his heels, lifts my ankles onto his shoulders and hammers into me. His eyes bore into mine with ferocity. "You are MINE," he grunts. "That means all your holes are mine."

"Yes... yours," I moan and close my eyes as the bliss builds. His possessiveness thrills me. I am his. My husband's cock fills my pussy to perfection; no other cock is better.

"Good," he growls and redoubles his efforts, slamming into me with such vigor I can tell I'm going to be sore tomorrow. I welcome the pain.

When he reaches down and slides his thumb past my asshole's tight ring of muscles, I groan from the unexpected pleasure. His voice is harsh. "I own this too."

The idea that I belong to him makes me go half out of my mind and my muscles tighten as I spiral towards my climax. "Ian... Ian... Yes... Ohhh god..." I'm practically screaming as he fingers my ass while his thick shaft pumps in and out of my pussy with hard, fast strokes.

"Fuck, Erin." Ian grunts and swivels his hips, drilling into me with a primal need as his thumb penetrates deeper.

Pleasure slams into me, and I feel as if I'm flying as a wave of ecstasy radiates throughout my entire body. It's a soul-shaking orgasm that sends me shooting sky high.

My husband goes wild when I climax, fucking me with abandon. He removes his thumb and grunts as he gives one last thrust and empties ropes of his sticky cum deep inside me.

"Mmmm...." I mumble as he collapses on top of me, nuzzling into the side of my neck.

He whispers, "You're the best," and a warmth steals over me.

I hold him tight, running my fingers gently down his back as our bodies cool down. My pussy is deliciously tender and tiny spasms of delight continue to ripple through me, but my brain is humming. I never expected him to fuck me so hard. Was it because I let Jace play with my ass? Maybe we both have secrets that turn us on.

We move onto our sides and I snuggle up against his chest. He pulls my hand to his mouth and kisses the pads of my fingers one by one. "I love you," he whispers. "So, you'll do it again—fuck other men? You want to be a hotwife?"

I nod. "Yeah, I'll totally do it again."

"Thank you."

I glance at his face. "For what?"

He kisses me tenderly. "Trusting me, indulging in my fantasy."

"I wanted to do it," I protest. He needs to know I didn't do this just for him. I wanted to fuck Jace and Matt.

He grins. "Yeah, my slutty wife loved getting it in two holes."

"Mmm, I did."

I bury my head in his chest and inhale his familiar scent. Shit, what a wild day it's been.

We're both quiet for a few moments until Ian shocks me when he pipes up. "I enjoy seeing this slutty side of you. If I invite my friend from the office over to fuck you, can I watch?"

Holy fuck, who is this man I married?

I thought fucking a stranger would satisfy my curiosity, but now I want more. Ian asking to watch is the icing on the cake.

I purr, "Yes, my love. I'll fuck whoever you want while you watch."

And it's true. I'm officially the ultimate slut and I'm going to get as much cock as my husband allows. It's time for a new chapter in our marriage, and I'm excited to see where this is going.

The End

THE SLUTTY WIFE'S VACATION

HOTWIFE EXPLORATION 2

LACEY CROSS

CHAPTER 1

As Sasha and I approach the entrance to the casino and hotel, I glance down at my outfit and smile. This weekend is going to be fabulous. My tight black miniskirt and low-necked, slinky blue tank top make me feel sexy.

I feel a little guilty for going on vacation without Ian, my husband. He's stuck at home while I'll be having fun and making questionable decisions. He insisted I go and enjoy myself. Plus, Sasha had a discount voucher for the hotel that was about to expire if she didn't use it right away. So, I need to stop feeling guilty that he isn't here with me; he loves me and wants me to have a good time.

As Sasha and I wheel our suitcases to check-in, she interrupts my thoughts. "What's on the agenda for this evening, hot stuff? We have time for a bit of gambling before dinner. Do you want to give the slots a go?"

"Sounds like a plan," I say.

Sasha and I have been friends for years, and she's like the sister I never had. We get along famously, and I share everything with her. Her sparkling personality brings lightness and joy into any situation—and she's the one who helped me become a hotwife.

A month ago, my husband and I agreed that if I found someone I wanted to sleep with, I should pursue it. The next day, I flirted with my cat's attractive veterinarian and became his plaything. Being double penetrated by him and his technician has been the highlight of my year.

Afterwards, my husband enjoyed the thought of watching me fuck another guy so much that he asked if I'd fuck his friend while he watched. Mmm...yeah, that was a wonderful night as well.

But that brings us to this weekend. Ian said if I wanted to, I could find someone to sleep with, but he had one request: he wants to watch over video chat. It's not likely I'll find someone to have sex with in the next couple of days, but Sasha knows the agreement. She told me if she needs to make herself scarce for a couple of hours while I get busy, just toss her twenty dollars and she'll entertain herself and play some slots.

She's so funny and supportive, and it almost makes me feel guilty that her husband isn't willing to share her. She sighs wistfully about how she wishes she could fuck other guys as well and tells me she'll just live vicariously through me.

The line for check-in is unusually long. Maybe they're all here on discounted vouchers. I survey the lobby while I wait for the cue to advance and notice an attractive man looking me over. Hmm, interesting. He's not being too obvious, and I receive a much-needed ego boost because he obviously likes what he sees. A pleasant tingle runs down my back, and when we reach the check-in counter, I'm sure my cheeks are rosier than usual. Sasha notices the guy too and wiggles her eyebrows at me as we give our names and a credit card to put on file.

As I'm handed my keycard, Sasha gives me a knowing grin and teases, "He was checking you out."

"Oh, please...no, he wasn't."

I play it off, even though I noticed his glances. I'm surprised he wasn't eyeing Sasha. With her beautiful blonde hair, striking blue eyes, and petite frame and big boobs, she usually gets most of the attention from men. Not that I don't clean up well. I'm attractive and feeling sexy tonight...and I'm the one who can actually fuck someone if I want to.

As we head towards the elevators, I'm still confused about why the hotel and casino are crowded. You'd think a discounted weekend would be empty, and that's why they were tempting people to visit. Hell, maybe we're all just cheap bastards who only visit when we can get the rooms at a reduced rate.

As we pass a conference room, a sign catches my eye and I stop abruptly. The sign is welcoming veterinarians to a conference. My eyes widen with shock, and Sasha turns around when she notices I'm not moving.

I point at the sign. "Seriously?!"

She laughs at my reaction. "What? Rumor has it you enjoy being fucked by hot vets. Maybe you'll find another one."

My pussy hums in delight at the thought, making me giggle in response to her suggestion as we continue towards the elevator. My slutty side is all set to take another ride on a cock that isn't my husband's.

When we get in the car, I push the button for our floor and mutter, "If there's a conference here this weekend, why did they give out discounts?"

Sasha shrugs. "Maybe you should stop questioning the universe and instead be excited about the possibility of fucking a sexy vet."

I give her a sidelong glance. "There're hundreds of rooms in this casino, not all with veterinarians. Plus, there are women here for the conference, too. I won't be able to tell which guys are vets—I'm no vet whisperer. There aren't any signs on doors telling us 'hot vet in here', right?"

"All I hear is you whining about being allowed to fuck whoever you want this weekend while I have to behave. Just pick the nearest smoking hot guy and tell him you've got a pussy that needs an exam and see how he reacts."

Oh God, she's nuts. We laugh as the elevator dings and opens on our floor. My spirits lift as we walk down the hallway. It would be fun to fuck a hot vet again. I'm just not sure how to go about finding one who wants me and will fuck me on video chat. Jace, my cat's veterinarian, wouldn't object to showing off on camera to Ian, but he's half a state away. We've texted a few times since I fucked him, and he's definitely looking to set up a playdate again while Ian watches, but the timing hasn't worked out yet.

Our hotel room is nice, but not lavish enough that we'd want to spend all weekend holed up inside. I'm sure that's calculated to keep us down on the main casino floor and spending money. We drop our luggage off, and while I'm in the bathroom freshening up, I daydream about fucking a train of sexy, muscular men. My husband didn't say I could fuck multiple guys this weekend, but he didn't say I couldn't either. I should probably find just one first before my pussy makes these elaborate plans and then gets disappointed. Once I find one, then I can ask Ian if I can have more.

I'm giggling to myself when I join Sasha back in the room. She glances at her phone. "About damn time. We need to hurry."

Jeez, we've got plenty of time to gamble. It's not like we're on someone else's schedule. I don't want to tell her I was busy daydreaming about being a mega slut this weekend, so I hurry and follow her out the door.

The first thing I notice as we enter the casino area is how many sexy guys there are. Yup, definitely an excellent selection to choose from.

Wait, why are there so many attractive men here? It's like the Twilight Zone and I'm in an alternate universe where all the men are hot and willing to fuck me. I wouldn't mind a portal to that universe.

Sasha nudges me, and I shake my head to clear my daydream. She tips her head towards a guy. "Hey, look at that ass. It's fucking yummy. Prime real estate. Do you think he's packing more than just that tight ass?"

Yeah, I wouldn't mind taking a bite out of those buns. I check out the guy's delicious looking ass while rolling my eyes. "You have the filthiest mind—he's hot, though."

The guy turns his head to look in our direction as if he knows we're discussing him. My body tenses with surprise and disbelief as I stare at Jace. What are the chances? The odds of us landing in the same place as Jace are slim to none, but here he is. Sasha squeezes my arm, and I have to pry my eyes off Jace to look at her.

She winks at me. "Have a good time tonight, Erin. Your husband said to tell you to not forget the video chat."

My mouth falls open, and she giggles as she strolls away through the slot machines. I'm rooted to the spot in shock, but my entire body lights up when Jace's velvety voice brushes against my ear.

"Hello, Erin. Are you going to be a good girl for me tonight while I fuck that sweet pussy of yours?"

Oh my god, yes. He doesn't need to ask me twice.

I spin to face him. "I can be very good."

He chuckles as he wraps an arm around my waist, tugging me closer. My mind races. Should I try to find out how he and Ian set this up now, or do I just take him up to my room so he can use me all night long? It only takes two seconds for my body to hum at his touch and for me to know what I want: fuck first...talk later.

Jace is just as sexy as I remember. He's in his late 30s with dark brown hair. He's taller than me, with a powerful, fit frame. I know exactly how well he's able to hold me down and fuck me hard, and my pussy flutters in response to the memory.

His deep blue eyes gleam as he smiles at me, and his hand skims lower, squeezing my ass. He leans forward and presses a kiss on my neck, teasing my skin with his lips before pulling back to whisper in my ear, "Let's take this party to my room. You've been a very naughty girl since our last visit. I'm going to need more than just your pussy tonight."

Excitement surges through me, and I suck in a sharp breath. Shit, Ian and I didn't discuss what holes could be used this weekend. Last time I was with Jace, he indicated he wanted to use my ass the next time he saw me. When I told Ian about it, Ian got so worked up by the thought that I didn't know if he'd be okay with it. I didn't bother asking about having anal this weekend because I wouldn't want to experiment with someone I don't know, but with Jace...mmm, I'd let Jace fuck whatever hole he wants.

Jace's lips capture mine, and we share a heated kiss that leaves me panting and wanting more. How the hell does he do this to me? I just have to look at him and I'm immediately in the mindset of being his fucktoy, wanting only to please him. If he asked me to do something, I would, without thinking. It's insane.

He grasps my hand and pulls me along with him towards the elevators. I'm assuming this was all planned and that's why Sasha was in such a rush, but I'll get the story out of her tomorrow. Jace mentioned going to his room and not mine, so I don't have to worry about Sasha. She's a big girl and can take care of herself tonight.

As we wait for an elevator, his fingers caress mine, sending ripples of joy down my spine. When the doors open, we're alone and he presses me against the elevator wall and ravishes my mouth as the doors close. Holy fuck. I melt into his kiss and lose track of time, forgetting where we are. He runs a hand up my inner thigh and under my black skirt. Since my skirt is tight, I can't give him as much access as I'd like, but I'm able to spread my legs enough for him to rub my pussy through my panties. I groan with pleasure. I want to feel him inside me—right now.

The elevator dings and comes to a stop. The doors open, snapping me back to reality. Three people are waiting outside, and my cheeks flush as Jace removes his hand from between my legs. There's no doubt about what we were doing. A woman titters and the two men smile at me as we pass them by. I silently wish them all good luck for the weekend and hope they get laid.

Jace pulls me along the deserted hallway, stopping at a doorway at the end. Instead of pulling out his keycard, he presses me against the wall and kisses me deeply while kneading my breasts with his massive hands. I can feel his hard cock through his jeans, and I don't understand why we're not in his room with his cock in me yet.

I push at him and give him my best sensual purr. "Take me inside. I need you."

He nibbles on my neck, and for a moment, I think he's going to ignore me. My head spins as a delicious shudder shoots through my body. God, he's intoxicating.

"First," he murmurs as he licks and sucks on my neck. "You have a choice to make."

"A choice?"

Like...which hole? A spark of concern zips through me because I don't know if I can make any decisions while my head is swimming. I want him to fuck me and not give me a choice.

He grips my waist and grinds his erection against me. I can hear the smile in his voice. "Yes. Do you want one or two...?"

His hands wander back to my breasts, and I'm confused. When he pulls on my nipples, I moan, "One or two what?"

"Cocks."

He swoops down to give me a bone-tingling kiss before I can reply. Am I hearing things? His hands slip under my tank top, and he lifts it above my head, exposing my black lace bra. My arms are in the air and he drops my shirt on the ground as he pulls the cup of my bra down to expose one breast before moving his lips to my nipple.

Holy fuck, we're in the hallway! I frantically glance both ways, but we're still alone. His teeth graze my nipple, making me forget that he asked me a question. Mmm, that feels amazing. His tongue flicks my nipple while he works the other breast out of its bra cup with his fingers.

Wait. Did he ask me about two cocks? My brain is mush from the pleasure of his mouth on my breast, and I try to form a sentence. "Two...two guys?

He grins around my nipple in his mouth and gives it a hard pull of suction before letting go to answer. "Matt came with me this weekend. He's in the room. Are we telling him to leave or stay?"

My mouth forms an 'O' as all thoughts drain from my head except for being spit-roasted by Jace and Matt again.

Jace laughs at my expression. "Your husband said it was your choice.

He'd love to watch you with us both, but you decide."

Holy fuck. If Ian wants to watch, the decision is already made. I'm desperate for both of them again, and Ian's been my only concern. My pussy gets wetter as I think about explode. My husband wants it after all. What else is a girl gonna do?

"So, Erin, what will it be? One or two?"

I wrap my arms around Jace's neck and press my lips to his. "Mmmm, two please!"

CHAPTER 2

I don't bother adjusting my bra, and Jace grabs my tank top from the floor. Excitement surges through me, and I feel like an absolute slut as we step into the hotel room. Had I known what was in store for me before the trip, I wouldn't have been able to sleep for days. When I get home, my sweet husband can ask for all the blowjobs he wants. He deserves many, many blowjobs.

I pause with my tits hanging out of my bra when I see Matt on the king-sized bed, naked and ready for us. His cock is hard, and he's stroking himself. His face lights up when he notices my bra pulled down, and he strokes faster.

What if I had said no to their proposition? That would have been a bit awkward, but let's be honest...I doubt anyone thought I'd say no. Hell, my husband probably assured them I'd pretend they were my favorite rollercoaster and ride them both all night long. And once Jace said my husband wanted to see me with two men, how could I say no to that? I snicker to myself. A girl's got to take one for the team occasionally to make her husband happy.

Matt is still impossibly sexy. He's in his mid-twenties, with short blonde hair and those yummy arm sleeve tattoos that still just do it for me. I'm more attracted to Jace just based on his being an older dominant man, but Matt is smoking hot. My mouth waters when I think of sucking his glorious cock again.

Jace presses up behind me and massages my breasts, pulling on my nipples and making my toes curl from the pleasure. Fuck, this is good. When he turns me in his arms and claims my mouth with a savage kiss, I moan against his lips as a wild, sharp need ripples through me.

His voice is rough with lust. "I want you on your knees, sucking my cock, but first you need to call your husband. He's waiting for you."

My legs nearly give out when I picture my husband sitting in the living room, staring at his laptop, his cock hard and aching as he waits for me to video chat. I bet he's stroking himself right now. Ian is an amazing lover and is generous in bed, but lately I've been the aggressor with sex. Now, he's taken charge, and this is a wonderful surprise.

Jace rubs his thumb along my bottom lip. "Go on, be a good girl and call him. I'm sure he's getting impatient."

Mmm, yes, I'll be a good girl. There's a dresser with a TV on it a good distance from the bed that will give a full view of the action. Setting my purse there, I dig my phone out and call my husband on video chat. I'm not surprised that he picks up immediately. When his face fills the screen, he's wearing a wide smile. A wave of love for him washes over me.

"Hi babe," I say and blow a kiss at the screen.

His eyes shine as he gives me a sly grin. "So, do you like your surprise?"

I pan the phone around the room to show him Jace, sitting at the foot of the bed, and a very naked Matt. "If you're talking about these two hot guys you arranged to fuck me tonight, then yeah, very good surprise."

"Good. Now it's time for you to show me how well you suck another guy's cock. Get your clothes off. I want to watch."

His words sizzle my brain, and it takes me a moment before I can think. Jesus, what has gotten into Ian? He's never this demanding. Yeah, I fucking love my husband.

I prop the phone up against the TV so it's facing the bed. I stand in front of it and cup my breasts. "Is this a good view?"

"Oh yeah, baby. Wonderful view." Ian rustles around, and I can tell he's doing something with his pants—probably opening them so he can stroke while he watches.

I giggle and blow him another kiss. "Enjoy the show."

He blows me a kiss back as I quickly kick off my shoes and unzip my skirt, letting it fall to the ground. I'm wearing black panties to match my bra, and I slow down to give the guys time to appreciate what they're about to have. I face the bed to tease them, rolling my hips and slowly peeling my panties down my legs. Ian moans his approval from the phone behind me.

It's a little weird that he's not in the room, but just knowing he's turned on makes this even hotter. I unhook my bra and throw it aside, cupping my full breasts and giving them a squeeze, watching as the men in the room react. Jace growls, his hand sliding down to squeeze his cock through his jeans while Matt moans and strokes his shaft more quickly.

Jace smiles, and his voice is low and commanding. "Now get on your knees and crawl over here. You're going to show us how good you can suck cock."

I feel a thrill of submission course through me as I sink to my knees and crawl towards the bed, my breasts swaying with each move. I stop in front of Jace and look up at him. "Should I start with your cock or Matt's?"

Jace chuckles, his gaze raking over my body. "Mine."

I lick my lips, my mouth watering as I kneel between his muscular thighs and reach out to unzip his jeans. I pull his cock out and grip his shaft firmly in my hand. With a slow, deliberate pace, I take him into my mouth, my lips sliding up and down his length. The taste of him is salty and sweet, a delicious combination of masculine muskiness and undeniable desire. As I lap up each drop of pre-cum, the sensation of him against my tongue sends pleasure zigzagging through me. It's too bad Ian can't see much from this angle.

Jace lets out a strangled groan, his hands fisting in my hair as he starts moving my head up and down his length. I take him deeper into my mouth, my tongue swirling around his cock. For a few moments, the only sound in the room is the wet sounds of me slurping on him.

Jace keeps guiding my head up and down his cock as he says, "Can you hear this?"

The sounds of me sucking on him fill my ears, and I assume that's what he's talking about. "Uh huh," I murmur around his cock.

"This is the sound of you learning to be a good girl."

My stomach flutters from joy, and a warm fuzziness floats over me as I bob up and down rhythmically. I want to be his good girl, and I'll do whatever it takes to get him to say it.

I can feel every throb of his cock, and I'm curious to taste him since I didn't last time. When his cock spasms, he pulls my mouth off him before he comes.

Looking up at Jace, I ask, "You don't want to come in my mouth?"

Jace shakes his head. "Oh no, I'm going to come deep inside that pussy of yours. Now go show Matt what he's been missing."

I crawl up on the bed and over to Matt, my heart racing with anticipation. He's leaning against the headboard, and I approach him from an angle that gives my husband a side view of my body. I want to make sure Ian gets to see the action since my back was to the camera while I was sucking on Jace.

I take Matt's cock into my hand, feeling the heat and weight of it as I slowly stroke him. Looking up at him, I ask, "What would you like me to do?"

Matt's eyes darken with lust. "God, I've been daydreaming about your mouth for weeks."

Shit, that's hot. I get a jolt of pleasure from him admitting he's been thinking about me.

As I sink my mouth down on Matt's cock, my lips stretch around the thick girth of it. I work my tongue, licking his shaft as I take him deeper into my throat. I get a moment of déjà vu as I think about how his cock tastes different from Ian's. It was the same thing I thought the first time I was spit-roasted by these two. But now that I have more experience sucking cocks other than my husband's, it's not as weird to have a unique taste in my mouth.

Matt's moans of pleasure fill the room, and when I feel his balls tightening against my chin, I almost giggle. He was stroking so much before that he might come quickly. I won't mind, especially not since he's been thinking about me all this time. He was probably stroking and imagining me sucking on him, and now he gets to enjoy the real thing.

When Jace moves behind me on the bed and rubs his cock up and down my wet slit, I moan my approval. Matt swears as he tries to hold back his orgasm. As I pull my lips off him, I stroke his slick cock, watching it swell and twitch under my touch.

With a swift movement, Jace plunges into my pussy. I cry out in pleasure as his cock stretches me out and fills me completely. Jace groans, his fingers digging into my hips as he pounds into me, his cock hitting just the right spot to drive me wild.

Oh...my...god. I give a long moan from the intense bliss before I suck on Matt's cock again. I bob my head up and down, trying to keep my movements synchronized so that every time Jace slams into my pussy, it forces Matt deeper into my throat. Matt's leg twitches, and I can tell he approves of what I'm doing. Saliva drips down his cock as I work him over, my fingers wrapped around his thickness as my mouth glides up and down.

I turn my head as best I can to make sure the phone is still upright. It is. I can only imagine how this looks to Ian. He's got a side view of me while I'm sucking on Matt and getting plowed by Jace. Too bad the phone is too far away for me to see Ian clearly. I'd love to see him stroking himself while another guy fucks me.

Jace draws my attention to what he's doing when he growls, "Do you like being a little slut for us?"

"Yes," I moan around Matt's shaft.

Jace continues to talk dirty. "Is that because you're just a filthy slut who wants a cock in all her holes?"

His words send a shiver of delight through me because it's true. I've been daydreaming about Jace fucking my ass for weeks now.

"Admit it," he demands darkly. "Admit you're just a filthy whore who wants to be used all night and have all her holes filled."

Fuck...I can't think when he talks to me like that, and my brain blips out as Jace hammers into me.

A sharp slap to my ass makes me cry out around Matt's cock. I lift my head off of him and grind back against Jace. "Yes. God, yes, just a dirty whore who wants to be used."

Jace says, "Good slut," as he fucks me steadily.

I focus back on Matt's cock, putting my lips around him and sinking down to the base. When his cock pulses against my tongue, I suck harder, and he explodes with a groan. I swallow his cum as best I can as it spurts down my throat. Now that I know I've made one guy come, I'm desperate to make Jace blow his load as well.

As Matt slips free of my mouth, I glance back at Jace. "Fill me. Please?"

"Not yet," he says.

Dammit, I want his cum inside me. My orgasm is building, and I know if I get his cum, it will tip me over the edge. My pussy is trembling and clenching around his cock.

"Please," I beg. "Come inside me. I want to feel it."

"That's a good girl," he chuckles. "Now get on your back. I want to get you off before I shoot my load into that sweet pussy."

Jace pulls out, and I want to scream with frustration. I need him to come so badly. I've never been this crazed for a man's cum before.

I practically dive onto the mattress and roll over. Once I'm on my back, Jace hovers above me and captures my mouth, his tongue tangling with my own. My entire body tingles from the pleasure as his hands roam over my breasts, massaging the soft globes as he deepens the kiss. I sigh, and he releases my lips as his mouth travels lower.

Trailing soft kisses along the sensitive skin of my neck, he lingers on my favorite spot, sucking and licking until I'm sure I'll have a hickey before the night is over. Fuck, that's hot. I want him to brand me.

I squirm beneath him, pushing my breasts against him, urging him lower. He's torturing me with his kisses, and I desperately need more. I want everything he can give me.

His lips finally land on my nipple, and he swirls his tongue around the taut bud, gently biting the swollen flesh. My pussy floods with wetness as I buck beneath him. I'm going to go insane if I don't come soon.

He glances at my face. "Patience, my little slut."

Oh, fuck this. I moan out my displeasure, and his mouth moves lower. He plants a row of kisses along my ribcage and navel before burying his face in my soaked pussy. I nearly lift off the bed as he sucks on my swollen clit, sending a rush of sensation throughout my body.

"Ohhhh, god," I cry out as he slides two fingers into my hot channel, finding just the right spot as he pumps them in and out.

I whimper, arching my back as the intense pleasure builds in layers. When his fingers speed up, it sends me over the edge. I cry out as I explode. Waves of ecstasy ripple through me, and he continues to suck on my clit, prolonging the pleasure.

After the last spasm subsides, I collapse onto the mattress. I lay limp while Jace kisses my inner thigh. He traces his lips along the soft skin until he reaches my knee before kissing his way back up my other leg. I'm quivering beneath him, my body thrumming with excitement, and I can't believe how turned on I still am.

His eyes burn with passion as he gets to his knees and positions his cock at the entrance of my pussy. He grins wickedly as he enters me in one hard thrust. I cry out at the exquisite pressure of my pussy adjusting to his thick shaft again. He stills for a second, and my breathing returns to normal while I relish the feeling of having him buried inside me.

I turn to look at the phone on the dresser and blow kisses towards my husband as Jace slides in and out of me. The erotic sounds of his cock thrusting in my wet pussy, combined with his labored breathing as he nears his climax, drive me wild. I look back at Jace as he hammers into me harder and harder, his thick cock pounding into my soft, wet pussy.

I wrap my legs around Jace and hold on to his shoulders as my climax builds. When Jace leans down to claim my lips, my toes curl and my whole body stiffens from pleasure. He groans, thrusting one last time as his warm cum splashes the walls of my pussy, triggering my release. A sharp pleasure runs from my fingers to my toes, and I moan and writhe as he fills me with his cum. My pussy spasms around him, milking him dry, desperate for every last drop.

Once my climax recedes, I can't help the delirious giggling that follows. Jace pulls out, rolls onto his side, and I relax. Fuck, that was good.

Matt chuckles. "Don't get too comfortable. You're not done yet."

What? I turn my head to look at him. He's erect again, his cock pointing towards the ceiling, begging for attention. Yeah, guess I'm not done yet.

Jace strokes my hair and tilts my face towards his. His mouth meets mine, and he kisses me with such intensity that it takes my breath away. My heart is pounding with anticipation, and I want nothing more than to have his cock buried in me again, but he has other ideas.

"Roll over like a good slut, and get on your hands and knees," he demands.

I do what he wants without hesitation. I'm just their fucktoy for them to play with. My pussy is throbbing and desperate for more. Oooh, wait. Now do I get it in the ass? Wait…I need to talk to Ian first. I can't have that.

Matt gets off the bed and moves to the other side so he can climb on behind me. I relax a little when I realize Jace didn't put me in this position to fuck my ass. Mmm, does this mean I get Matt's cock in my pussy tonight, too? I'm not sure why I assumed I'd just be sucking him off like I did before.

This is like a double treat.

"Time for your second round. Do you think you can handle both of us, or are you too tired?" Jace asks, teasing me with the possibility that they might stop.

"Bring it on."

Hell, I feel like the biggest slut at the moment, and I could probably take on an entire battalion of hot veterinarians. I'm insatiable, and I love how dirty I feel. I revel in my new hotwife role.

I wiggle my ass and look over my shoulder at Matt. "Fuck me, please. I want you inside me."

He presses in behind me, wrapping one hand around my waist and using the other to guide the tip of his cock to the entrance of my pussy.

My core melts at his touch. I need him. "Please...hurry."

As he eases his cock into my pussy, I'm flooded with pleasure. I moan loudly as I push back against him, needing all of him inside me. Ohhh, god. They can use me all night long if they want. I'll be the best fucktoy there is.

"Fuck me hard, please. Don't be gentle," I beg.

"Like this? Is this what you want?" Matt pants out as he hammers into my pussy.

I grip the comforter as he rides me. I can feel my breasts bouncing with every thrust. I'm not sure I can answer him, so I moan, "So good."

My husband loves it when the pleasure short circuits my brain and I can't talk. I really hope Ian is stroking as he watches. I want him to be enjoying this because I'm not sure I want to stop being a hotwife. This is wonderful.

Jace kneels next to the bed so he's directly in front of me, and his thumb brushes my lip. I know what he wants. I part my lips, and when his thumb enters my mouth, I suck on it. He watches me intently as I reach for his cock. I grasp it in my hand, and his eyes flash with lust.

His voice is low and strained. "I'm going to fuck that pretty mouth of yours."

Mmm, yes. When he moves his cock towards my mouth, I flick the head with my tongue and he growls in appreciation.

He strokes my hair and whispers, "Keep being a good girl."

He holds my head in place as he pushes his cock past my lips and into my mouth. I can taste myself on him, and it's like licking an Erin lollipop. The thought makes me giggle, but I quickly become distracted by how deeply he's fucking my throat.

Jace's eyes are focused on his cock driving in and out of my mouth, and when I look up at him, the corner of his lips lift. It's obvious that he likes this, and my pussy spasms when I realize I'm going to get another load of cum from both of them.

Holy shit, I love my life, and I adore Ian for arranging this. I can't believe he planned it all out for me.

Matt's thrusts intensify, and I know he's going to come. He gives several last thrusts before he empties his seed into me. I let out a muffled moan, and a burst of pleasure shoots through me as my orgasm takes hold. My entire body trembles as my muscles contract, waves of rapture rolling over me.

When my tremors stop, I continue sucking Jace's cock as Matt climbs off the bed and sits in a chair. My arms are shaking, but I want Jace to finish down my throat. The way he's making short and quick thrusts as I suck harder tells me I won't be disappointed.

Jace grabs the sides of my head, pumping furiously into my mouth as my lips slide over the thick length of his cock. My mouth is stretched wide open, and it feels so dirty to have my lips wrapped around him, especially knowing my husband is watching. I love being the center of attention.

Jace lets out a low growl as his cock erupts. He spurts into my mouth, and I do my best to swallow the hot, salty liquid, but there's so much some drips out. It runs down my chin when he withdraws from me. He drops his forehead on mine as we pant for air.

"You've been such a good girl," he whispers, and I flush at the compliment.

When Jace gets off the bed, I collapse onto my stomach. Oh god, I feel so used. It's glorious.

Jace puts on his jeans before picking up the phone to talk to my husband. "Ian, I want you to see how pretty this little slut is when she's used and well fucked. Do you like my cum all over her face?"

The only noise coming from the phone is a strangled groan. Jace angles the camera at my face as he wipes his thumb across my chin, clearing up some of the mess. I smile at the camera, knowing I probably have a goofy grin. I'm cum drunk from all the fucking and enjoying my slutty facial. I've never had so much cum in one night before, and I can't say I mind one bit.

Jace puts the phone in my hand, and I'm looking at Ian. My voice is a soft purr. "Hi, baby."

"Hello, my sexy wife. I love you. I fucking love you." Ian's voice is shaky, and I'm pretty sure he just blew a massive load while watching.

I giggle. "You look happy. Did you like that?"

Ian smiles at the screen. "Yeah, it was awesome."

I blow a kiss at the camera, my chest flooding with warmth. This man is perfect. I have no clue how I got so lucky, but I'm thrilled he enjoys watching me with other men.

"You better be ready to get fucked the moment you walk in the door," Ian teases me.

I give a soft laugh. "Okay, I can't wait to see you and give you all the attention you deserve."

My pussy spasms at the thought of my husband driving his cock deep inside me. I'm going to show my appreciation for everything he's done by riding him for days when I get home.

"I can't wait. Have fun, baby. We'll chat tomorrow." Ian ends the call.

I stretch out my legs, enjoying how relaxed my body feels.

Matt and Jace have been quietly cleaning up. Now they sit in the chairs, dressed and looking at me with smiles.

Matt is the first to speak. "Thank you again, Erin, for a wonderful time."

Jace nods in agreement. "You were amazing and a good girl."

My body hums from his praise. "Yeah, maybe we can do this again at home while my husband is in the room watching?"

Matt's eyes spark with interest, but he turns to look at Jace for direction.

Jace's lips twitch with a smile. "Sounds good to me. I'll contact Ian and set something up."

They stand, and I can't resist sitting up and pulling them into my arms for a hug. We're laughing, and I give them both a quick kiss before getting cleaned up and dressing.

Jace escorts me to my hotel room, making sure I can get in with my key. Before the door opens, he pulls me into his arms for one last deep kiss. I melt against him as his tongue sweeps through, caressing and exploring my mouth as he trails his hands up and down my back. He's turning me on again, and I want to fuck him in the hallway right now.

When he releases me, we share another long gaze. I don't think he wants to go, but he forces himself to say, "Goodnight, Erin."

I step through the doorway, turning around to give him a little wave. "Goodnight, Jace."

As I close the door, I realize Jace didn't even try to fuck my ass. What's up with that? He makes me admit I want it in all my holes and then doesn't even give it to me? A warmth of wetness from my pussy makes me giggle. Yeah, fucking dom guys. He's going to make me desperate for it before he gives it to me. I mean, it's not like he was going to get it tonight without me talking to Ian, but he should have at least tried!

Sasha isn't in the room yet, and I assume she's still playing slots. I'm giddy and laughing at myself as I fall onto the bed, my entire body drained from all the orgasms.

Yep, Ian deserves blowjobs for days. I'm the luckiest slut alive.

The End

Slutty Wife Unleashed

Hotwife Exploration 3

Lacey Cross

CHAPTER 1

My hands are over my closed eyes and my heart races with excitement as my husband, Ian, leads me to the spare room. He claims he has a surprise for me, and I can't wait to see what it is.

"No peeking," he reminds me.

I giggle. "I'm not looking, but don't let me trip."

"We're almost there," Ian says and stops walking.

My curiosity gets the better of me and I finally ask, "Can I open my eyes now?"

He's been keeping me out of the spare room for an entire week. All he said was that he was creating something for me.

"Sure. You can look," Ian says with a smile in his voice.

I drop my hands and blink twice to clear the spots from the sudden change before gasping in shock as my jaw drops. The bed is gone, and in its place are two long couches against the walls, new side tables, and in the middle of the room, a shiny silver pole sticking up from the floor.

Holy shit, Ian got me a stripper pole! I squeal with happiness and throw my arms around him. I've been talking to him for a year about wanting to take pole dancing lessons, but I never imagined he would actually want one installed in our house.

He kisses me soundly and laughs at my delight, and when I let go of him,

I examine the rest of the room. There's new lighting in the ceiling and a stereo and speakers. He went all out. The floors were already hardwood, so he didn't need to do anything different with them, but he installed a wall of mirrors across from the couches.

"This is amazing. Thank you so much!"

He grins broadly, amusement twinkling in his eyes as he hugs me. "I hoped you'd like it."

Yeah, this room isn't going to be open to family when they visit anymore. I'll just tell them it's now a storage room, and keep the door padlocked if I have to.

Ian's never done anything like this for me before, and my hands shake with excited energy. I approach the pole and study where it's attached to the ceiling.

My voice is bubbly and I start talking fast. "Is it secure? Have you tested it out already?"

When I imagine Ian dancing around the pole to test it, I smile. My sweet husband probably wouldn't dance for me, but I know he'll enjoy watching me.

I pull on it and I can tell it's going to hold my weight. I can't help teasing him with a sly grin. "So, what made you decide to do this?"

As if I didn't know. He just wants to watch his slutty wife pretend to be a stripper.

Ian leans against the wall, crossing his arms against his broad chest. His eyes darken with desire. "You became a hotwife because I asked you to, so I wanted to do something you've been asking for."

I open my mouth to protest that I'm not fucking other men just for him, but he continues. "Plus, you'll look sexy sliding all around that pole. I'd be crazy not to encourage that."

Well, that seals it. There will definitely be a lot of shows for him.

Ian sits on the couch, reaching for a bag I didn't notice before from underneath a side table. "There's more to your gift, too."

More? He motions me over to him as he fishes something that looks suspiciously like lingerie out of the bag and hides it in his lap. As I get closer, he lifts his hands up to reveal a see-through black teddy. Yeah, that seems more like a gift for him. Hell, everything so far is a gift for him, but it's something I've wanted, so it's sweet of him.

I purr at him. "Ohhh, you're going to wear that for me? I initially thought you said you got me a gift, but you're the one who's getting a gift here. The teddy would look sexy on you."

He chuckles, shaking his head and pulls me into his lap. "Not me. You'll be wearing it when Jace and Matt come over next weekend to watch you spin around that pole for us."

My brain freezes for a moment as a delicious tingle spreads over my body. Jace is my cat's veterinarian that I fucked one wild day at his office while his technician, Matt, used my mouth. Later, Ian arranged a surprise for me to fuck them both on a casino trip while he watched over video chat. I envision swinging around the pole in the black teddy with the three men staring at me, waiting for me to get naked and fuck them. Holy shit, he already arranged it?

Oh god, what if I suck? My heart races with unease. I haven't had any training. What if I make a complete fool of myself?

I can feel my face flush as I bite my lip and hesitate. "Shouldn't I learn how to first?"

He rubs my arm in soothing circles. "Baby, you're gorgeous, and whatever you do is going to be fucking sexy. All you need to do is swing around it a bit and you're going to have us drooling."

Hmm… I climb off his lap and test out the pole again, twirling around it to see how it feels. He settles back onto the couch and smiles at me. He's not worried about a damn thing.

Hooking my leg around the pole, I arch my back and wink at him. "Like this?"

The bulge under his jeans is noticeable, and his voice is husky. "Yeah, that works.”

He's probably thinking of me in the teddy. I get a jolt of courage and try a few more poses, working out the best ways to balance with my leg hooked around the pole. Pretty soon, I'll be able to do some decent choreography. I wonder how much dancing the men expect me to do?

Unhooking my leg, I turn to Ian and strike a pose that I think might be seductive. I run my fingers through my hair, thrust my tits forward, and put an extra roll to my hips. I slowly approach the couch and pull off my shirt, glad that I'm wearing one of my favorite bras, a wisp of purple lace.

“And what else should I do that night with you guys?”

His eyes wander down to my breasts, and knowing he's turned on by what I'm doing gives me a zing of pleasure straight to my clit.

“I'd like to watch you have sex with them,” Ian replies, his voice growing rough. “But only if you want to.”

Oh God, he's nuts. As if I'm not going to want to fuck their brains out once I get worked up playing stripper for them. I hold in my giggle as I unbutton my jeans and peel them down my legs.

I tease, “Watching me suck another guy's cock gets you hard, huh?”

A flush creeps up his neck, betraying the heat stirring within him as he watches me step out of my jeans. I turn my back to him, then bend over to pick them up. When I stand and glance over my shoulder, I catch him adjusting his crotch.

I lean down, sticking my tits in his face as I take off my panties. He hums in approval as I toss the underwear to the side and straddle him. His erection nudges my soaked slit through his jeans, and I grind on him briefly before sitting in his lap. I hope he didn't plan on wearing these pants all day. He's going to be a mess when I'm done with him.

My hands roam over his muscular arms, loving how strong he is. And he's all mine. I lean in close to kiss him, flicking my tongue against his.

Pulling back a fraction, I murmur, “I love the stripper pole. Thank you.”

He grins, and I can tell he's satisfied that I appreciate his gift.

I nibble at his earlobe. "So why isn't your cock inside me yet?"

In an instant, he flips me over and I squeal in surprise as he presses my back against the cushions. Oh shit, I guess he's taking me at my word. As he fumbles with his pants, I wrap my arms around his neck and I giggle at his enthusiasm.

He guides his cock into my pussy, and I moan as I lift my hips off the cushion to meet him. Mmm, this is perfect. When he's fully sheathed in my pussy, he grazes my neck with his teeth as he fucks me. With each plunge into me, a sharp jolt of bliss travels from my pussy to the rest of my body. I tangle my fingers into his thick brown hair as his thrusts grow harder.

He nuzzles my neck before trailing kisses down to my shoulders, leaving tiny bites along the sensitive flesh. Fuck, I love that. My husband is such an amazing lover, and knowing how hot he gets at the idea of sharing me is the icing on the cake of our marriage.

As I near my orgasm, Ian pounds into me, speeding up, and I can tell he's fighting to hold back his release. The pressure builds, and my climax rushes over me like a dam bursting free, taking away every thought as the pleasure rips through me. I shudder through my orgasm, my pussy clamping around him.

He thrusts one last time before he erupts, moaning into the purple lace covering my breasts. We're panting for air when he collapses on top of me, his cock still twitching inside of me.

Ian mutters against my shoulder, "Christ, you drive me wild."

I run my fingers through his hair and giggle. "Just wait until the weekend. You haven't seen anything yet."

I'm too content after my orgasm to be worried about my lack of dancing skills. Ian's the most wonderful husband, and a quickie was just what I needed tonight.

CHAPTER 2

Ian had invited Jace and Matt to come over Saturday evening, and I've been watching pole dancing tutorial videos online to prepare. Every day, I sneak into the spare room to practice when Ian isn't around. It helps me relieve some of the stress about my impending performance since I still don't feel graceful on the pole. It will be different with guys there, though, and hopefully the sexual energy from everyone will make me not feel as self-conscious.

By Saturday lunchtime, I'm nervous, but also crazy turned on. I can barely eat, but I know that my body needs the fuel because I'm hoping to get a nice workout tonight.

After I eat as much as I can get down, I spend a long time pampering myself with self-care. A warm bath with a peach-scented body scrub loosens my nerves. I let my mind drift, imagining how tonight will go. Are the guys going to just watch me dance and then fuck me? Will they make me choose between them, and are Matt and Jace going to both fuck my pussy, or will Matt just want my mouth again? I have no idea what the agenda is, but just thinking about them using me as their fucktoy has me flushed and turned on.

Wait. I jerk upright, causing water to splash over the side of the bathtub. Anxiety sets in as I realize I needed to have a serious conversation with

Ian about anal sex. Jace keeps saying he's going to use my ass, but Ian got possessive when I told him about Jace fingering my backdoor.

Yeah, fuck, I need to talk to him. I climb out of the bathtub, and force myself to slow down long enough to slather lotion all over my body. As much as I want to race out there to chat with Ian, the other guys won't be here until evening, so there's plenty of time.

Once I'm sufficiently moisturized, I put on my silk robe and hunt the house for my husband. I find him on the couch in the living room, watching a football game on TV.

I snuggle against him and give him my cutest, "Hi."

Ian pulls me into a sweet kiss before replying, "Hello, love. You smell good enough to eat. Did you enjoy your bath?"

"Mmm, yes. I'm nice and relaxed."

I'm only half fibbing. My body is relaxed, but my mind is keyed up about tonight and the conversation about anal sex.

Ian kisses the top of my head. "Good. I can tell you're still a little tense. Remember, it's only for a bit of fun tonight, no big deal. If you want to stop at any time, then let me know. I'll toss the guys out and we can watch a movie together."

Yeah, right, I don't think I'd ever stop for a movie when I have three guys willing to fuck my brains out.

I keep my voice light. "Um, we need to talk about what happens if one of them goes for my butt. I mean, I can say no, but you know how I get…"

He chuckles. "Babe, I already told them they can have any hole but that one."

Uh, he did? Fuck. Knowing he discussed what holes of mine they can use makes my head swim, but my stomach ties in knots from disappointment. Yeah, I'm totally a slut who wanted it in the ass tonight. I take a few seconds to get my thoughts sorted, and my words burst out in a heated whisper. "But what if I want it?"

He glances down at me with surprise. "Do you?"

My face warms as I shrug. Why is it so difficult to talk to my husband about my sexual needs? This should be the one guy who I can tell anything to, and yet I'm still embarrassed about my submissive urges and wanting to be treated like I'm just three holes to be used.

"How about this…" Ian kisses my head again before continuing. "Let's experiment with that ourselves first, and then I'll decide how I feel about someone else fucking your ass."

A thrill runs down my back and my nipples harden. Oh God, this is so damn dirty to be discussing. "Like today before they get here? Right now?"

He snickers softly. "No, before next time."

Oooh, next time! I sigh and snuggle closer to him. "That sounds good."

After a second of silence, he murmurs into my hair. "Erin, I want you to be happy with everything that happens, but just remember this is supposed to be fun for you, too."

"I know." I fiddle with the collar of his shirt as a warm feeling of being protected fills me.

He continues, "I love you so much, and you're my priority. So be honest and tell me if you need something different, okay?"

My heart squeezes with emotion, and I swear I'm the luckiest woman in the world to have a husband as thoughtful as Ian. "I will. Promise. I love you, too."

He plants another soft kiss on my head and wraps an arm around me as we settle into watching the rest of the game.

CHAPTER 3

My hands tremble as I stare at myself in the bedroom mirror. The black lace teddy that Ian bought me highlights my breasts and hugs my curves. It's thin lace, and if I bend over, Jace won't need to do a hole check tonight. He'll be able to see everything clearly. Thank God I took the time to tidy up the lawn down there. The ensemble is slutty as hell, and it makes me feel like I'm about to be served on a silver platter to three hungry lions. Mmm, not that I'd mind if the lions ate me.

I pull my long brown hair up into a ponytail and fasten a black choker around my neck. To complete my look, I slide on my sluttiest black spiked high heels. Luckily, I've been practicing dancing in them. The instructional videos were really helpful, and I've got a few moves down. It will be enough to please the crowd, and something tells me this is going to be an easy audience to win over.

As I adjust my breasts in the cups of the teddy, my heart skips in anticipation. Obviously, I've been the center of attention before in my banging sessions with the guys, but tonight is different. All eyes really will be on me from all angles with the mirrors on the wall, and I'm trying not to psych myself out.

The doorbell rings, and Ian calls down the hallway, "They're here."

I smooth my hands over the black lace, feeling nervous but eager. Ian and I meticulously planned out tonight's events. He'll greet our guests, get them drinks, and lead them to the spare room. He'll turn on some music and when the moment is right, I'll make a grand entrance and give them a performance they'll never forget. Easy, right?

Just thinking about it has my core tightening, and a surge of warmth rushes through me. Hopefully by the end of the night, I'll have a good story for my best friend Sasha. I promised to tell her all the slutty details. Oooh, I'll send her a picture while Ian gets the guys settled.

I grab my cell phone and snap a photo of myself in the mirror.

Erin

> The men are here and they are about to get the full stripper treatment.

Sasha

> #jealous. You better give me all the details tomorrow.

I giggle at her response.

Erin

> I will. Promise!

It really is too bad that her husband won't share her like mine will. At first, I didn't want to become a hotwife, but now that I am one, it's fucking fabulous. Sasha struggles with monogamy and she would have loved to have a husband as open as mine. I'll just make sure to tantalize Sasha with all the filthy parts so she can imagine it was her instead. Hopefully this doesn't include a sad tale of me ending up flat on my face as I try to twirl around the pole in these heels.

Oh God, why did I agree to do this? My anxiety bubbles up and before it turns into full-blown panic, I take a few deep breaths. Okay, stop it. I can do this. I shouldn't be worrying. This is just going to be some sexy fun with the men. I keep giving myself a pep talk as I leave the bedroom.

The nervousness fluttering in my stomach increases the closer I get to the spare room. I can hear upbeat music playing through the door. I don't pause to give myself time to worry. As I open it, I see Matt and Jace are sitting on the same couch, lounging comfortably, while Ian is on the other one. Their focus immediately shifts to me when I enter.

Jace is just as sexy as I remembered from my trip to the casino. He has a powerful, fit frame, and he's wearing blue jeans and a green T-shirt. His presence dominates any room he's in, and I can feel myself growing damp between the legs as I meet his deep blue eyes.

The men stare at me with undisguised hunger as desire simmers low in my stomach. My face grows warm, but I refuse to look away. I'm a sexy slut and I'm going to own it tonight.

I keep my head high as I saunter over to the pole with what I hope is a confident stride and give them my best seductive tone. "Hi, guys."

"Holy fuck, Erin, you're killing me in that outfit," Matt groans as he squirms in his seat.

I focus on Matt and my nipples harden when I see he's wearing a T-shirt that shows off his muscular arms with their full sleeve tattoos. My attraction to Matt always surprises me because he's in his mid 20s, which normally would be too young for me. But his enthusiasm when he fucks me is endearing, and I love being a super slut and worshipping his cock while Jace drills into me from behind. Mmm, yeah… I'll take some of that tonight.

When I peek at my husband, I see that Ian's eyes are dark pools of desire, and I can feel my pussy growing even wetter. I've been turned on all day, but his appreciation works me up even more.

Jace stands up and approaches me, and my body buzzes with neediness. I want his hands all over me. Or better yet, his cock inside me.

He steps behind me and wraps his arms around my waist. When he nuzzles my neck, I hold my breath and my nipples pucker. I press back against him and wiggle my ass as he presses his lips behind my ear in a gentle kiss.

He whispers softly, "You look stunning."

I remember to breathe again as I spin in his arms. His eyes burn with passion as his gaze bores into me, and I feel my heart race with a sexual hunger. The room fades away as I focus on his obvious desire for me, and I forget all about my fear of performing.

With one hand on my waist and the other on my lower back, he pulls me closer to him. His lips brush against mine softly before deepening the kiss, his tongue exploring every corner of my mouth. As I melt into his touch, the last of my worries and doubts disappear from my mind. I can feel his passion for me through every movement of his hands and lips, and it makes me feel alive. They really won't care what I do, and they'll love every minute of it. I have to trust this, and I want to have fun with them, too.

I moan as Jace cups my breast with his hand, and his thumb brushes against my nipple. I'm spellbound as the fingers of his other hand caress my inner thigh. Oh, fuck. I shiver with delight as he grazes my wet folds through the teddy. I wish the fabric wasn't between us. If he doesn't stop, I'm going to beg him to fuck me before I even dance for them.

I tear my mouth off his with reluctance. "Don't you want a show?"

Jace laughs. "Definitely. Work your magic." He gives my nipple one last tweak before stepping back.

I glance towards the couches as Jace sits back down. Matt grins enthusiastically, and his intense stare heats me up. Ian looks like he's already half out of his mind from lust, and I mentally smile. Yeah, Ian is enjoying watching me with other men in person instead of over video chat.

I turn and take a tentative grip on the pole as I survey my surroundings. The music pulses through me, my clit throbbing in time to the beat. A surge of power washes over me, and I push away the last of my reservations. I know what they want, and I want it too.

As soon as my hold on the pole tightens, my body sways in a sensual rhythm. I glance at my husband and admire how sexy he is as he sits back with a clear bulge in his pants. The show might be for all the guys, but Ian is the one I want to please the most. I'm going to fuck the pole the way I want to fuck my husband.

I dance in a slow, undulating wave around the pole, using my entire body for effect. Each time my face passes the guys' line of vision, I smile seductively and lick my lips.

Their expressions encourage me, and I tug down the strap on my right shoulder to tantalize them. Matt shifts, and I can tell he's trying to make more room in his pants for his growing erection. Feeling the lust emanating off the men makes me feel like a goddess, and I continue to move to the music, letting it flow through me. I was concerned I was going to be awkward the entire time, but I feel fluid and graceful. Dancing for them gives me an erotic high I didn't expect.

Jace smiles wickedly, and I can tell he wants to tear my teddy off and bury his cock deep inside me. But he just has to wait. I pull the strap on my arm down farther until it falls down, and I tease them by showing off the upper swell of my breasts.

I twirl and give the guys a view of my ass as I drop low to the ground and work my way up the pole. I throw them a little extra shimmy before I turn around and hook my leg around the pole as I lean my body against it. The music is inside me, pulsing through my veins, and there's no stopping me now. I thrust out my hip and give them a view of the sheer panel on the front of the teddy that barely hides my pussy.

All of them have huge grins, and I want to give them more. I focus on my dancing for a few moments as I rock to the beat and jiggle my ass at them. As I peer over my shoulder, I notice the men leaning forward slightly, enraptured, and I'm shocked at how powerful I feel. They're craving every little movement I make. I'm a sexual enchantress enslaving them with my body.

I hook my leg around the pole again and rotate around it. Every nerve ending in my body is alive and the music washes over me like a living thing.

I rub my body against the pole as I let the song fill me.

Matt wipes the sweat from his forehead as he leans forward. "Christ, she's sexy."

My heart races as my face burns from the rush, but I need more. I want the men so crazed for me that they come over here and fuck me. It's time to show them more skin.

I slip my straps off my arms and turn my back to them as I roll the garment down far enough to expose my entire backside. Jace whistles as he gets a good eyeful. I bend over to remove my heels, and then I slide the teddy all the way off.

I pause a moment to compose myself, but when I look back, my pulse jumps as the intensity of their gazes sends a jolt of heat between my legs. I'm naked except for my black choker necklace.

Twirling slowly around the pole, I allow them to feast their eyes on my entire body. My clit throbs, driving me wild, and I let myself go completely. The erotic atmosphere intoxicates me, and it's like I'm a totally different person. The end of my ponytail tickles my shoulders as I dance, and I trace my hand lightly up my side before grabbing the pole and swinging my legs in front of me. I thrust out my chest and point my toes as I arch my back to give them a good look.

Jace leans forward and when he licks his lips, my confidence skyrockets. I love teasing him, and knowing he's thinking about fucking me hard sends a ripple of pleasure straight to my clit.

As the song ends, I position my back towards them, grab the pole and open my legs. When I bend over, I hope someone takes the hint. I'm ready to be fucked.

Another song starts, and I stay bent over and reach a hand between my legs to play with my clit. The guys have a full view of my fingers as I tease myself and dip two inside my pussy.

I hear a rustle as one of the men stands up, and I'm not surprised to look over my shoulder and see Jace behind me. He brushes my hand aside and takes over. I close my eyes as a delightful buzz zings through me. He expertly strokes my swollen nub while easing a finger into me, and I wiggle my hips against his hand in encouragement. I cry out when he slides a second finger into my wet pussy.

My lips part at the delicious sensation and I moan, "Yes."

Jace spanks my ass cheek while circling his thumb over my clit, and a jolt of pleasurable pain shoots up my spine. He moves his spanking hand to push on the small of my back and forces me to bend over more as he adds another finger, stretching my pussy lips open.

Ohhhh god. I whimper in ecstasy as I push against his fingers. Fuck, I need to come. My entire body is aching for release, and I thrust back on him, begging for more.

Jace's voice is gravelly with need. "You're so greedy for it. Tell me you're desperate to come for me, my sweet little slut. Tell me you want my cock buried so far into you that you can feel my balls slapping your ass."

Matt gives a sharp inhale of pleasure, and I look under and behind me to see Ian's reaction. Ian white-knuckles the arm of the couch and his chest is visibly rising and falling. The tent in his pants is bigger than I've ever seen before.

Knowing that my husband is turned on is all I need to allow myself to sink further into submission. I'm ready to be used, and surrender myself to the moment. Jace strokes his hand along my back as he waits for me to answer, his fingers inside me slowing down.

"Please don't stop," I whimper, then beg, "I want it. All of it. Please?"

He rewards me with fast circles around my clit, driving me mad and forcing me to hold onto the pole tightly for support. I pant as I lift my ass up for more.

Jace coos at me. "You're so lovely when you're desperate. Good girl."

Pleasure washes over me and I bite my lip to stifle my cries, but they escape anyway. Matt gets off the couch and drops to his knees right beside us as I tremble on the brink of orgasm.

Matt bends forward, grasping my chin with a strong grip, and demands, "Open your mouth."

My head swims at the command and my lips part automatically. As Matt pulls his cock out of his jeans, Jace pushes me onto my hands and knees. Matt aims his cock at my mouth, and I moan a second before he slides it inside. I try to swallow him all down, my lips stretched wide to accommodate his girth. He buries in deeper, pushing past my gag reflex, and I concentrate on licking and sucking on him.

Jace smacks my ass with a loud crack, and Matt hisses when I squeak from delight and my throat convulses around his shaft. The feeling of my wet mouth makes Matt go crazy, and he becomes rougher than he ever has before.

I shift my gaze upwards and lock onto Matt's dark eyes as he fucks my mouth. There's a wildness in his eyes that matches how I feel, and I welcome whatever they want to do to me. I'm focused on Matt, so I'm surprised when Jace slams into me from behind. The shock of pleasure is so intense, the room spins as I cry out around Matt's cock.

Jace hooks his elbow around the pole for leverage and sets a punishing pace, hammering into me relentlessly as his balls slap against my sensitive clit. He doesn't seem to be holding back. My body is overwhelmed by their combined force, and I give into the intoxicating feeling of being used for their satisfaction. It's pure bliss.

Matt holds my head in place and uses my throat, his cock thrusting in and out rapidly. I'm so busy being ping-ponged between the guys, I barely have time to wonder what Ian is doing. He knows he can stop this at any time, but I'm not expecting him to. He set this up tonight, and he's the one who wants the full experience of seeing me fucked by two men at once.

Matt's cock pulses in my throat a second before he blows his load. He groans loudly as spurts of hot cum coat my throat. I struggle to swallow it all down, and when he pulls out, some escapes and drips down my chin. Knowing I'm going to be a mess makes me feel like an even dirtier slut, and

I revel in the sensation.

Jace grabs my ponytail and I yelp as he jerks my head back. The bliss spikes through me and the joy builds in layers. He drives into me, riding me, and my toes curl as ripples of pleasure wrack my body until I can't take it anymore. I cry out as I orgasm, and he fucks me through the waves of euphoria in an unrelenting rhythm.

I expect him to keep fucking me until he comes, but he suddenly stops and removes his cock, pulling me back against his chest until I'm upright on my knees. He kisses my neck as he holds me in place by my hair. I'm still shuddering from the aftershocks of my orgasm and my brain is mush.

"Does our little slut like being used?" Jace growls as he releases my hair.

I moan out, "Oh god, yes, please don't stop."

I'm still floating when Ian appears in front of me, dropping to his knees to pull me into a scorching kiss. Ooooh, god, yes! I'm desperate to suck my husband's cock and I claw at his jeans, trying to get to him, but he grabs my wrists and holds them between us.

Between deep kisses, he says, "Erin, baby, you're so gorgeous. But I just want to watch tonight."

Watch? My husband must be half crazy, but I know he'll fuck me later, so he'll still get to come. Jace drags the tip of his cock over my slick folds and teases my clit with the head.

I moan out, "Yes, my love."

Holy shit, having Ian in the room is more intense than I expected. Last time he was watching over video, and while that was hot, it's nothing compared to touching him while another guy's cock is poised to press into my pussy.

Ian breaks off the kiss and stares at me with lust-filled eyes. I can tell he's getting a major rush from viewing the show and my eyelids flicker from pleasure as Jace sinks his cock into my sopping wet hole. He feels even thicker than he did a few moments ago, and it's exquisite as he massages every nerve ending deep inside me. I'm drunk on pleasure, and I lean forward to grasp my husband's arms as Jace slams into me.

Jace's voice is rough when he starts in with the dirty talk. "Are you enjoying being used like a fucktoy?"

"Yes," I whimper, closing my eyes in ecstasy as he pumps into me, fucking me furiously.

He's brutal as his cock jackhammers me. I cling to Ian like I'm afraid he'll disappear if I let go. I need the connection, or I might shatter into a million pieces.

My breasts swing with every whack against my pussy, and Ian takes advantage and moves a hand down to play with my nipples. I cry out as he tugs on my nipple and the delicious thrill drives me higher and higher towards another orgasm.

Jace reaches in front of me and finds my clit with his fingers. Sparks of electricity travel down my thighs, and my pussy squeezes him hard. I'm almost at the peak of ecstasy and I just need a bit more. I ride out the building tension.

Just when I'm about to orgasm, Jace's voice is deep and commanding. "Come for us."

My pussy contracts with such force, it startles me, and my orgasm sweeps over me, short-circuiting my brain as I cry out. My pussy milks Jace's cock as he pounds into me until a rumble vibrates in his throat. He explodes, releasing ropes of sticky cum deep inside me.

As we shudder together, the pressure subsides, and my legs lose their strength. I'm shaking and clinging to Ian to keep myself from collapsing on the floor as Jace pulls out.

Ian scoops me up and carries me over to the couch. He lays me down on my back and sits by my head, stroking my hair.

"Are you done, baby? Have you had enough?"

My brain is fuzzy and it's difficult to answer, but as I look across at the other couch, Matt is sitting there stroking his cock. He's hard again.

I want him.

I need him inside me, filling me and using me as Jace did. I open my mouth to beg Matt to fuck me, but the words stick in my throat.

I manage to choke out, "Please, I need more."

My husband gives me a fierce, approving smile. "You heard her. She wants more."

Matt doesn't need any more prompting, and he gets up and Ian moves over to the other couch to watch. Matt settles between my legs, hikes one of my knees over his shoulder and drives into my cum-soaked pussy. He fucks me hard, hammering away at me, and I cry out as pleasure ripples from my fingers to my toes as he ravages me.

His speed picks up and I think he's about to blow his load when he slows down, edging me closer and closer to my orgasm again. I can feel each thrust hitting a wonderful spot inside me and it drives me crazier than the fast pounding did. I'm about to beg him to speed up when Jace kneels by my head, his cock hard again.

I open my mouth eagerly, and he guides the tip past my lips. I can taste myself on him, which almost shuts my brain off from how filthy it is. I'm sucking on a guy who just fucked me while my husband watched. What type of woman does this?

A slutty hotwife, apparently.

Me.

I love the freedom of letting go and taking pleasure. My body feels boneless as I let go, surrendering to them again, as Jace thrusts deeper. All I can think about is them fucking me in both holes. Maybe someday I'll get every hole filled at once. Would I then get a medal for being a total slut? I'd giggle if my mouth wasn't busy.

Matt shifts positions, pushing my knees close to my chest, and being curled up while the two guys fuck me sends me over the edge again. My throat is full of Jace's cock and it muffles my cries, but my body convulses from the intense pleasure. My juices explode around Matt's cock, and knowing I'm making a mess of everything makes this filthier in a wonderful way.

Fuck, this feels amazing. The high of having Jace's cock in my mouth and my pussy being used by Matt drives me wild. When Jace comes a second time, he pulls out of my mouth fast to paint stripes of his semen all over my face. I feel like a complete whore, and that's exactly what I craved tonight and didn't even know it.

Ian murmurs from the other couch, "Shit, that's sexy."

That comment unleashes Matt, and he slams into me hard enough that my tits bounce. My voice is hoarse as I beg him, "Just do it! Use my pussy. Come in me!"

Matt groans out, "Yessss," and his fingers dig into my hips so hard that I'm pretty sure he's going to leave marks. But I don't care, I want the visual reminder of tonight.

The thought tips me over the edge again and I spiral out of control once more, calling out, "Oh god, I'm coming… fuuuuuck…"

My pussy clenches on Matt's thick shaft, and he stills as his warmth floods me. We're locked together, and the aftershocks of my orgasms zip through me with mini-contractions. He sighs with satisfaction and slowly withdraws his softening cock, dropping my legs back to the couch.

Holy fuck, that was insane.

Ian gets up and comes over to my couch to sit down and pull me into his lap. I shiver as I feel cum leaking out of me. Yeah, I'm probably getting his jeans dirty, but I don't care. I rest my head against his shoulder and realize I'm getting cum on his shirt also. Oops.

Ian's voice holds a hint of amusement. "Now are you done?"

"For now," I tease him in a sing-song voice. I'm definitely not done with him, but I am done with the other two.

He strokes my hair as he murmurs into my ear, "I'm going to put you in bed and then talk with the guys, okay?"

I nod and wrap my arms around him, melting against him. He smells good, and the comforting scent of home and safety is like a blanket that wraps around me. My eyes drift shut, and I'm so exhausted, I think I could fall asleep on him.

Ian stands up with me in his arms and I feel cum-drunk as I call out to Jace and Matt, "Thank you both for the good fuck."

Jace's deep laughter is the last thing I remember.

CHAPTER 4

I must have fallen asleep, because when I wake up, I'm under the covers in the middle of our king-size bed with just Ian. I roll over to face him.

"They're gone?"

Ian strokes my cheek, smoothing wisps of hair that escaped my ponytail off my face. "Yes, we're alone now."

My heart expands in my chest with all the love I feel for him. He's the best husband in the world and I'm the luckiest woman on Earth. "Thanks for setting all this up, my love."

He cups the side of my face with his warm palm. "Of course."

When he leans forward to kiss me, my whole body tingles, and I coo with happiness. I deepen the kiss, telling Ian I want more without using words. He responds by wrapping his arms around me, rolling onto his back, and dragging me on top of him.

He's already naked, and I wiggle until my pussy is against his cock. I don't have the energy to reach between us, so he takes over and I shift just enough for him to hold his cock steady and guide it into me.

I moan as he fills me. My face is inches from his and he pulls me closer to him so he can kiss me. I love my husband, and there's nowhere else I'd rather be. The man knows me so well, and he supports every fantasy and desire I have. I'm grateful and I want to make him happy, too.

I rock against him as I whisper against his lips, "You take care of me better than anyone in the world and I love you, Ian."

"You deserve the best in the world. I would do anything for you. I love you, too."

As I lift my hips and start a gentle rhythm, I pepper his face with soft kisses. His hands find mine and we lace our fingers together as we make love. This is one of my favorite types of sex with Ian, and my body starts tingling from the delicious friction.

I'm so worked up that my orgasm comes quickly. I gasp out as the pleasure erupts and my pussy contracts around Ian's shaft. He wraps his arms around me and we cuddle for several minutes, neither one of us moving, as aftershocks quiver through me.

Ian trails kisses from my ear down to my collarbone, sending a wave of fresh desire through me. I pull up a little so I can feel him sliding into me, and my body lights up when he moves a nipple to his mouth, sucking on the sensitive bud. A bolt of pure bliss flashes through me as he nibbles the tip and then runs his tongue around the areola before taking my nipple fully into his mouth and sucking it. My hips buck against his and I moan out his name.

Ian gives my tits lavish attention as I continue riding him. It feels wonderful, but I know he needs to come. He deserves to come.

I can feel the heat building between us, his hands roaming all over me, igniting every inch of skin. Switching my movements, I sit up straight and grind down hard on him, feeling every inch of him filling me. He grasps my hips, guiding me with each thrust, his breathing becoming more ragged as he approaches his climax. His eyes roll into the back of his head from pleasure as I increase my tempo. I'm so wet, I can hear the slapping of my pussy against him as I ride him.

I can feel the tension building in Ian's body as he nears his climax. He's panting and muttering nonsense phrases. He's so far gone, anything is going to make him explode.

I slow down for a moment, and he looks up at me, startled. I grind my pussy into his groin and wiggle around on top of him before going back to bouncing on him. With a smirk, I toss my head back and brace my hands on his abs to give myself a little more leverage as I ride him faster and harder than before.

"Come for me... come for me... come for me," I chant.

With one final surge, Ian's moans reach a fever pitch and he loses control, exploding inside of me. His cock spasms and his cum mixes with the other two guys' as his leg muscles quiver from pleasure. I ride him a few more moments before collapsing onto his chest.

Ian sighs, "Christ, babe, you drive me nuts."

I snuggle on top of him and giggle. "Same thing, next weekend?"

He groans in mock protest. "Anything for you, my love. But before next time, there's an ass I need to claim."

I get a naughty surge of happiness and I tilt my head and smile at him. "I think that can be arranged."

We kiss softly before I scoot off of him. My body is worn out from tonight's activities and my eyes drift closed. I'm warm and content, but my mind fixates on next time. Is he really going to let Jace fuck my ass?

I really want it. I'm such a dirty slut, and I wouldn't have it any other way... and apparently, neither would Ian.

A First-Time Backdoor Experience with My Husband

When my husband gets off work on Monday, I'm prepped and ready for him. It's time for him to fuck my ass. I've been sending him dirty text messages all day to get him worked up, and he told me to be in bed when he gets home. I follow his directions, and I'm waiting for him when he arrives.

Well, okay, he might not be expecting this. I'm naked and in the middle of the bed, leaning back on a pile of pillows with my knees bent and my feet flat on the mattress. My hand is between my legs, and I'm circling my finger around my clit when he walks in. I'm horny and worked up enough that I could easily get myself off before he touches me. I can already feel my arousal dripping down the crack of my ass.

Ian stands by the door and locks eyes with me, and his smile makes my stomach flip. I can see he's hard under his slacks and I grin at him.

"Did you have a good day at work, my love?"

He starts taking his shirt off and almost growls at me. "If you consider being hard and trying to hide behind my desk all day a 'good day,' then, yes."

Oooh, nice. My pussy clenches and I give him a mock pout. "Oh, poor baby. That does sound rough."

The corner of his mouth twitches and I speed up the motion of my hand, enjoying the swirl of pleasure in my core.

Once he finishes removing all of his clothing, he opens the dresser drawer where we keep the lube and I can tell the moment he doesn't find it.

"Are you looking for this?" I hold it up for him to see. I want to giggle. Did he expect me not to get it out? "You wanted me ready."

Ian laughs and as he climbs onto the bed, I get onto all fours, presenting my ass to him. I'm a filthy girl who wants her husband to claim her ass. I've waited long enough.

Ian puts one hand on each ass cheek, caressing them. "You're sure you want this?"

"Less talking, more ass fucking," I demand.

He chuckles and leans forward to get the lube. Ian's touch sends a tingle of excitement to my clit, and I can't believe I'm so excited to let him take my ass. The thought of him possessing it turns me on more than I thought it would. It makes me feel like his dirty little slut, and I love it.

After spreading lube between my cheeks and working it in, he also adds some to himself. My husband kneels behind me as he rubs his lube-coated dick up and down my crevice, and I groan from pleasure. I push back against him.

When the head of his cock nudges my tight entrance, Ian says, "I don't want to hurt you."

I look at him over my shoulder, frustrated that he won't just shove it in. "Please. Please. Fuck my ass, Ian, and make me your little slut."

I never realized how much calling myself a slut could make me soaking wet, but it turns out, I really enjoy being called dirty names, even if I'm the one doing it.

He bites his bottom lip as he lines up the head of his cock again, and this time he presses in hard and keeps going. Fuck, it hurts for a second, but the pain is instantly replaced by a delightful fullness. A fiery heat races through me, and all I want to do is throw my ass back and take Ian's entire length.

I want Ian to really fuck me. My pussy aches with need and my arms shake. I need this.

Grabbing two pillows to support myself, I lower my chest to the bed and surrender my ass to him. The feeling of submission overwhelms me. Until the time I fucked my veterinarian and he called me a 'good girl,' I didn't realize how much I craved submission in the bedroom.

This moment with my husband sinks me further down into submission than I've ever gotten with just him. I'm giving my husband everything I have, and my brain shuts off as I embrace the animal instincts running through my body. I need my husband's cock. He said this hole was his. Now he needs to claim it.

He grasps my hips firmly to steady me as he sinks his cock into me. Once Ian is in up to the hilt, he stops and gives me a moment to adjust. His hands run all over my ass before he strokes my lower back in soothing patterns until the muscles in my butt unclench.

It feels different from him fucking my pussy, in a good way. The sensation is intense and new and a little scary. But with a little patience, I'm able to relax fully as Ian keeps stroking my lower back.

He must be able to sense the moment I fully give in and open myself to him, because he starts thrusting. I moan softly as the pleasure builds. Being this open and vulnerable has me crazed and desperate for him to give me relief.

"Rub your clit for me," he demands, and I snake my hand between my legs.

My clit is swollen and covered in wetness as I swirl my fingertips around it. The hunger builds fast and my clit throbs as the warmth in my core turns into an inferno as the overwhelming fullness spreads throughout me. The fire rages within me, consuming me from the inside out. I need this. I crave this. It's been a long time coming. I need his cock in my ass. I need it like a drug, and I've been starved of it too long.

But here it is. Here he is, claiming my ass so thoroughly, owning me like no other.

I cry out, "Yes! Yes! Give me more. Harder."

His fingers dig into my hip bones as my husband loses himself to the moment. He fucks me harder and my breasts sway beneath me, slapping against one another.

"Tell me I'm yours," I gasp out.

Ian sounds like he's almost growling as he fucks my ass hard. "You're mine. This ass belongs to me."

He picks up the pace and I stroke my clit faster, right on the edge of bursting into flames. "Take it! Take it, please, make me your good girl, ohhhh god."

Ian embraces the moment with me. "No one gets to use this hole unless I say so. It's mine."

"Yes, yours!"

A powerful climax explodes through me as I hear him affirm that I belong to him, that he owns my ass and controls me. My world focuses down to just Ian and the possessiveness of his powerful hands as he drives into me. I scream with my release as wave after wave of scorching pleasure erases everything outside of us.

The first pulse of Ian's seed blasts me as he cries out in triumph, "Fuck, fuck, you're mine."

Each hot rope of cum is like liquid love filling me, and I focus on his pleasure. It satisfies a deep part of my soul to submit myself fully to him. Tears trickle down my cheeks, and I collapse onto my stomach as he pulls out.

Holy fuck. I've never felt this level of intense connection with him before.

Ian rolls onto the bed next to me and our chests heave as we try to calm down. After a minute, he pulls himself off the bed and I can barely think enough to wonder what he's doing as he heads to the bathroom.

When he comes back, he has a wet washcloth, and I moan softly as he cleans me up. I'm still floating in my post-orgasmic bliss.

He discards the cloth in the laundry basket and lies down on the bed again before pulling me against him.

"Fuck, that was good," he murmurs as he kisses my head.

I can only hum in response as my eyes close. As I mentally drift, his fingers caress my shoulder, and a slight smile tugs at the corners of my lips. My ass is a little sore, but in a delicious way that reminds me I was claimed by my husband.

This means that when the time is right, he might let Jace fuck my ass... maybe.

I'm such a lucky, slutty wife.

The End

SLUTTY WIFE ON EDGE

HOTWIFE EXPLORATION 4

LACEY CROSS

CHAPTER 1

My heart pounds as my husband, Ian, maneuvers our car into the empty parking lot of the veterinary clinic. Ian isn't giving me many details about why we're here, but he promised me a Saturday afternoon I'd never forget. What fantasies await behind those shuttered windows? Ever since my first visit to the clinic where my best friend told me to ask about "special services," my life has taken a wild, thrilling turn. I fucked my cat's vet Jace and his technician Matt multiple times, so a trip to the clinic while they are closed only means one thing...I'm getting another shot at their gorgeous cocks.

A shiver runs down my spine as I remember the last time I fucked them. Ian installed a stripper pole in our spare room, and I gave the three men a private dance. Jace and Matt's strong hands gliding over my skin as I danced for them was erotic as all fuck. The pole still stands ready in our spare bedroom, but today isn't a dancing day. I have a feeling this playtime will lead us somewhere entirely new and deliciously taboo—hopefully with a cock in my ass by the time we're finished.

Since that first day with Jace, he's been teasing me about fucking my ass, but he's never tried. This past week, Ian laid claim to my ass in the most wonderful way. The feeling of him filling my ass was completely different from anything else I've experienced. I've never felt so loved and wanted.

Ian turns off the car and grins. "Are you ready, baby?"

I nod, breathless with excitement and unable to find my voice. Is it bad for me to hope that Jace is finally going to fuck my ass today? I'm new to anal sex, and I've only done it once, but with Jace's continual teasing about it, I'm turning into a wanton slut over the idea.

Since Ian lovingly and sexily claimed my ass for his own...there's a chance he'll be willing to share it. I've been wet all day just thinking about it, and I almost touched myself earlier today to take the edge off. But I was a good girl and held back. I'm so worked up, I bet whatever orgasms I have today are going to be amazing. I'm ready for the men to use me any way they want to and the ache between my legs as I get out of the car proves how much of a slut I am. Thank God my husband loves the slut he married.

As we walk across the parking lot, Ian surveys my chosen outfit approvingly. After a lot of debate this morning, I picked out a sea green skirt and simple matching tank top. Lots of easy access.

He steps behind me and rests his hands on my hips, pulling me back against him and making me stop walking. "I love that color on you."

I can feel his hardness against my ass, and I shimmy my hips to torment him. He makes a happy sound deep in his throat and holds onto me and grinds against my ass. Hell, at the rate he's going, do we even need to go into the vet's office? He could push me up against the side of the building and fuck me right here.

"You know," I say, "if you had told me what was happening today, I could have made sure I was dressed correctly."

He kisses my neck. "What you have on is perfect. You look beautiful."

I laugh and wiggle my ass again. "Thank you. But I want to look more than beautiful."

"Oh?"

"Mmm hmm." I press my ass against him harder. "I want to look like your slutty wife."

He laughs. "Don't worry, Erin. You always look like that because that's what you are."

Oh fuck, why is that so hot? I know he only means it in the most loving way. He and I both enjoy my newfound wild side. I whimper and lean into him. He's so hard against me, and all I want to do is grind on his cock. I think of how he felt in my ass again, how full and new it felt, and my clit aches.

He pushes my legs apart far enough that he can slip his hand down the front of my skirt and finger my pussy. What the hell? We're in the parking lot! I glance around and relax when I realize the side of the building is hiding us from the main street.

He makes a little growling sound against my ear. "You're so wet already. You're looking forward to this, aren't you?"

I rock against his hand as his fingers circle my clit. I'm already in a little bit of a submissive headspace just from the thought of what Jace and Matt are going to do to me, and the tone of Ian's voice makes me slip a little farther. "Mmm, yes. I've been thinking about it all morning."

"Good," he says, his fingers stroking me faster. I whimper and move my hips with him. Just feeling his hardness against me makes me think of being on all fours on our bed while he fucked my ass for the first time earlier this week. Everything is making me think of a cock buried into my ass. It would feel so good if he did that again—or if he decides to let Jace do it. I can't stop hoping that his whole plan today is to let Jace use whatever hole he wants.

He nips at my earlobe. "You're going to love what we have planned for you."

When he pulls my skirt up over my hips, I'm aware of the cold air on my ass, and I get lightheaded thinking of how it felt to have him filling me up. I really should protest that we're in the parking lot, but my head is too fuzzy and everything feels too good. His fingers keep moving on my clit while his thumb presses softly against the fabric of my panties, as if he's trying to rub my asshole.

It's such a good tease, and I whimper again. "Ian. I want you so much, are you sure you don't want to just go home and fuck me?"

I don't really want that, and I know he doesn't either, but he's making me desperate.

"I'm just making sure you're ready for all our cocks."

"Fuck, you know I am." The swirling of his fingers is hypnotic as heat grows in my core and my pussy clenches. If he keeps going like this, I'm going to come all over his fingers.

He pulls his hand away. "I guess we better get in there and see what happens."

I whimper at the loss of his fingers. I know he has to stop toying with me or else I won't get to fuck Jace and Matt, but I still wish he would have pushed me against the building and taken me right here. I want all three of the guys to use me today, and that includes my husband. I want to be the slutty wife of his dreams.

"Please," I say, wiggling my ass at him again, but he laughs and gives me just the lightest, most playful swat before pulling my skirt down.

"Patience," he says, shaking his finger at me.

I sigh. "Fine."

When Ian makes up his mind about something, there's no changing it. That's why I haven't tried to beg him to let Jace fuck my ass. If he decides to share me, he will. But if he does decide to...I'll give him a private dance on that stripper pole every night I live.

Chapter 2

We walk into the double glass doors together. My entire body is buzzing, and after Ian's little stint in the parking lot, I'm even more ready to beg for someone's cock. Ian's been delighting me with surprises ever since I became a hotwife, and all my experiences with Jace and Matt have been amazing. Whatever they have planned for me, I want it.

Matt greets us at the door as we walk up. He gives me a long, appreciative look, his gaze tracing all my curves. His greeting is warm and makes me melt. "Hi, Erin."

He's younger than Jace. His short blond hair and deep-set grey eyes are almost cute, but the full sleeve tattoos he has on both arms make me shiver. It gives him a raw and very male energy that makes me appreciate his stamina and strength. I'm not usually attracted to younger guys, but Matt is sexy enough that his age doesn't matter. Slut Erin just likes smoking hot guys.

Matt closes and locks the door behind us and starts pulling down the window shades as Ian and I move to the center of the waiting room. Just being back here at the veterinarian clinic makes my breasts tingle. Shit, am I going to get turned on every time I bring my cat to the vet now? Just being here and knowing that the guys are going to use me makes me sink down into my submissive headspace even more. I feel pliant and ready to be used.

I'm going to do whatever they want, like the dirty slut I am. Let's get this party started.

When Jace walks into the waiting room from one of the back offices, I take a moment to admire him. I'm very aware of how his tall, well-built body can make me feel. He has a commanding presence, and he exudes a strength that makes my whole body respond...and I love it when he calls me a good girl.

Both Jace and Matt are wearing blue scrubs, but Jace has a white lab coat on over his. There's nothing about their clothing that should be sexy, but they're so hot it makes saliva pool in my mouth. Maybe I'm Pavlov's dog and trained to want them now. I'll do all sorts of tricks for a long, hard treat.

I want Jace to call me a good girl.

And I really want him to fuck my ass.

Jace gives me a long look that takes in all of my curves. I pose a little and push my hip out, trying to show off. I bet he's remembering how sexy I looked twirling on that stripper pole. That was the night where his teasing about taking my ass inspired Ian to finally claim that hole for his own.

Fuck, I really hope Ian is ready to share.

"Hello, Erin."

Jace's deep, velvet voice makes my head swim in the best way. I want him and Matt to use me and make me their mindless slut.

"Hi, guys." Butterflies swirl in my stomach, but I'm more turned on than nervous. Even though I don't know what's going to happen next, a part of me is loving the suspense. This is the best way to drive me wild with desire.

"Are you trying to look innocent in that modest outfit?" Jace gestures at my skirt and t-shirt. "Because it isn't going to work. I remember the black lace teddy you were wearing last time I saw you."

I flash a flirty smile at Jace. "Nope, that would be silly. We all know what I want."

He moves closer to me, smiling so warmly. "Yes, we do."

When he pulls me against him, his scrubs can't hide how hard he is against my thigh. "We all know you want to be spit roasted again while your husband watches." He pushes a strand of my long, brown hair behind my ear gently. "Are you ready to be a good little slut and do as you're told?"

My knees go a little weak as I imagine sucking on his cock, and I purr a lusty, "Yes."

"Good girl." He gives me a long, passionate kiss. As our tongues twine together, I throw myself into the kiss and plaster my body against his. The longer he kisses me, the more needy I get.

Right when I'm about ready to try to ride his thigh, he steps back. "Get on your knees like a good fucktoy."

Jace's words are sharp without being mean, and I kneel immediately. The tiles are cold, but I don't care. All I want is to be a good girl so they will give me their cocks and fill me full of cum.

Matt and Jace don't waste any time. They push their scrubs down just enough to free their gorgeous cocks. Both men are huge, thick, and veiny. Matt is longer than Jace, but Jace is so thick it makes me salivate. I want to suck on them and get fucked by them both. This is the fourth time I've played with them, and I know how wonderfully full I feel when I'm stretched out by them, both in my mouth and pussy.

I can feel how wet my panties are, and it almost makes me laugh. Thank god I wore them today. I'd be a mess already without them.

Jace takes control. "Open your mouth like a good fucktoy and suck on our cocks."

His command makes me dizzy as I part my lips and stick out my tongue. Am I going to suck on them both at the same time? Jace and Matt step close, and I wrap a hand around each of their shafts. It's show time.

Leaning forward, I stretch my mouth as wide as it can go so I can engulf the head of Jace's cock. He gives me just long enough to swirl my tongue around the bulbous tip before he thrusts forward, filling my throat. He pushes past my gag reflex and holds me there. I groan, my throat working around his cock. He tastes different from Ian, and that turns me on even more. It's a dirty reminder that someone's cock is in my mouth and it's not my husband's. I know Ian wants this for me—for both of us. He loves me, and that's why he shares me. He gets hot watching me with other guys, and I get to be a dirty slut and get multiple orgasms. It's a win/win.

I bob on the cock in my throat and stroke Matt's shaft in the same rhythm.

"Fuck." Jace's voice is strained, and I feel a sense of pride. I'm a good cocksucker if he sounds like that.

He puts his hand on the back of my head, forcing me to move faster. I stroke Matt to match the rhythm, and Matt's breathing gets heavy as he jerks against my palm.

When Jace pulls back and his cock slips from my mouth, I immediately turn to lick the head of Matt's cock. It's salty with pre-cum, and Matt shoves his cock into my mouth harder than Jace did. I have to work to keep up with him while Jace continues to control the movement of my head. There's no chance to pull back and catch my breath.

Matt groans as he slams into my throat. I can feel how tense he is, and I try to push down harder, eager for his cum, but Jace pulls me off Matt's cock. Fine, take away my treat! I get my hand back around Matt and continue stroking both of them.

I expect Jace to shove his cock back into my mouth, but instead, Matt steps to the side and Ian moves in front of me. His cock is out, leaking at the swollen tip. Oooh, what's this? I didn't know Ian was going to participate today. This is slut wife heaven.

My pussy clenches from desire as I suck on my husband. Having a third cock in my mouth within minutes pings the naughtiest side of my brain. I want to be the ultimate slut for them.

I sink onto Ian's cock with just as much joy as I took the other men's. Jace holds onto my head and pushes me down fast and hard. I can barely breathe, and I don't care. My brain shuts off, and I become just a hole for them to use. Ian's cock is leaking on my tongue, and I want to keep sucking mindlessly until he blows his load down my throat.

Jace keeps a hold of my head, moving me from one cock to the other like a filthy slut who's just there to get them off. The longer it goes on, the more I want to be that. All I want is for them to explode in my mouth as their ropes of cum mix together and become too much for me to swallow. I want it dripping out of my mouth and running down my chin until I'm covered in cum.

Before any of them come, Jace forces me to stop. He pulls me off, and I gasp, filling my lungs with air. I put on makeup this morning, but when I see a smudge of pink on Jace's cock, it tells me that my face is probably a messy disaster. I love it.

Jace hums low in his throat as his thumb brushes my bottom lip, smearing my lipstick even more. "Such a gorgeous fucktoy."

A bolt of lust zips through my core as I stare up at the men. If Ian preplanned this all with them, my wonderful husband knows me better than I thought.

CHAPTER 3

Jace's grip is firm on my upper arms as he hauls me to my feet. My nipples harden in response to his commanding voice.

"Strip for us," he orders.

I reach for the hem of my shirt without thinking, ready to pull it off as quickly as I can. The sooner I'm naked, the faster I can get their cocks in me.

"No," he says in a firm tone that startles me.

I pause with my arms crossed over my body and look at him, waiting.

"Strip like you're getting ready to swing around a pole for us. Give us a show."

Pleasure pulses in my veins. Now I know what he wants. I give all three of them my sexiest smile before pulling my top up slowly. Matt makes happy sounds as each inch of skin is revealed. Their eyes on me sends lightning bolts of delight through my body. It reminds me of the other weekend when I really was dancing on the pole for them and how powerful I felt knowing I had them all under my spell. When I get my tank top off, I give it a little twirl and let it fly across the room.

I'm a little showier when I remove my skirt. Turning around so my ass is facing them, I rotate my hips in a slow circle. My firm ass is one of my best assets, and the extra exercise with the stripper pole only accentuates my curves. I want all the men thinking about my ass.

God, this is so filthy.

I hook my fingers in the waistband of my skirt and drag it slowly down my hips as I continue to bounce and jiggle my ass. When my skirt and shirt are off, I turn around, striking a little pose. My arms are behind my head, elbows out, and my hip is cocked to one side. The bra and panties I'm wearing are a matching set in lavender. The balconette lace bra barely covers my nipples, and the bottom is a wisp of silk that has me hyperaware of my ass.

Jace's eyes sizzle with heat as he looks at me while Matt groans, "God, Erin. You're so fucking hot."

Jace and Matt exchange glances, and Matt nods before heading towards a back room. Those two seem to be up to something, but the way my pussy is buzzing, I enjoy the mystery of everything today.

Jace gives me a speculative glance. "We're moving. Follow me."

When I take a step, he holds his hand up. "On your hands and knees."

A blush works its way up my body. "On my..."

He nods and his voice is like steel. "Now."

I do as he says, dropping down and getting on all fours, ready to follow him. The cold tiles bite into my knees, giving me a perverse pleasure.

"Good girl. Now crawl."

He takes a few steps towards the room Matt disappeared in. I slowly follow him, knowing that Ian is behind me and watching my ass. Why is this hot? The floor looks clean, but this is a veterinarian clinic so is it really? Crawling on a potentially dirty floor is degrading...which makes me even wetter. This is what it means to be their fucktoy—to obey.

My panties are damp and I bet Ian can see the wet patch. Just knowing I'm being watched has my pussy begging for one of their cocks inside me. They better not make me wait much longer.

Jace stops at the door to a small office and steps aside, gesturing me in first. "Go on. I want to appreciate the view."

As I crawl past him, I put a little extra shimmy in my hips. I want his eyes on my ass. I want him thinking about fucking me. About taking control of the hole he hasn't shoved his cock in yet.

"Mmm, so sexy," he says, and I shake my ass again.

He gives it a tiny smack, just enough to make me jump. I'm on my hands and knees in what looks like Jace's personal office. Matt is sitting in the desk chair, and Jace hovers behind me. I hear Ian come into the office, and when I glance over my shoulder, Ian leans against the wall and crosses his arms. I can tell he's prepared to enjoy whatever is coming next.

"Now, we're going to play a game," Jace says, and my eyes snap back to him. He strokes my ass, and I whimper before he continues. "We're going to use you."

His fingers slip down, dodging the hole I want the most and teasing the opening of my pussy through my panties. I moan and push back against him, but he doesn't press his fingers into me.

"We're going to take everything we want."

Lower, and he's teasing my aching clit. If someone was in my mouth while Jace was rubbing my clit, I bet I could come in two minutes.

"But one thing. You don't get to come without permission."

That startles me. I glance back at him, confused.

"You heard me," he says. "You're a greedy little fucktoy who is here for our pleasure."

My head is spinning. Oh god, I need his cock, and I'll beg as much as I have to.

Jace moves my panties aside, pushes two fingers into my aching pussy, and I moan from the pleasure. I'm not sure how much more of this teasing I can take without a cock inside me.

He finger fucks me slowly. "What are you thinking about, Erin?"

"What?" It's difficult to talk when my mind is fuzzy.

"Are you thinking about how good this feels?"

I'm shivering with need, and every stroke of his fingers is a shock to my clit. "Yes."

"Are you thinking how desperate you are for my cock?"

When he rams his fingers into my soft flesh roughly, I cry out. "Yes—fuck, yes."

He spins his fingers around so that his thumb is pressed against my clit. "You better be ready to beg, and you better hope I'm in a giving mood. I might just fuck you and leave you a desperate, wet mess."

I don't know if he expects an answer to that, so I stay quiet as his fingers quickly bring me close to coming. I push back harder, desperate to feel him inside me as deep as he can go. I just need a little more...

He pulls his fingers out, and I whimper as the swirling pleasure fades. Jesus, that's mean. The ache in my pussy doesn't go away, and I wiggle my ass. "Jace..."

"Before you get more, you're going to make Matt feel good," he orders me.

My brain parrots it back to me. Make Matt feel good. Okay. I crawl towards Matt, and all I can think about is being a good fucktoy and making him come.

While I was distracted with Jace's finger in my pussy, Matt stripped naked. His cock protrudes from his lap, thick and heavy. He's stroking it lightly, and it's fully erect for me.

I settle between his knees and take him into my mouth. I've given him a blowjob so many times I'm starting to know what he likes. Swirling my tongue around the tip, I clean up the pre-cum leaking out of him before applying just the right amount of suction as I slide his full length into my throat.

He groans and starts to fuck my mouth, his hips moving fast. I don't get to control the pace. I try to relax my throat and stay open for him as he holds onto my head and takes control. Every stroke is a lightning bolt of delight straight to my clit.

When Jace pushes my panties aside again, it's the only warning I get before he slams balls deep into my pussy. I cry out from the pleasure, but the sound is muffled by Matt's cock.

"Does that feel good, my sweet little fucktoy?" Jace's voice is a little strained, and I revel in knowing I'm giving him pleasure. I try to moan that yes, it does feel good, but my words are garbled. Matt hisses from the vibrations against his shaft, and I give up on talking as I throw myself into giving Matt the best blowjob of his life.

Jace hammers into me, and being trapped between their cocks switches something off in my brain. I really am their fucktoy right now. The only thing that would make this better is if Jace was fucking my ass, but this is close to perfect.

The pleasure builds in layers as I ping pong between the men's cocks. Every thrust from Jace shoves Matt's cock deep into my throat. I imagine both of them coming at the same time, and it almost tips me over the edge.

A stinging spank jolts me back to the moment as Jace growls, "You better not come without permission."

Heat swirls in my core as Jace drills into me, riding my pussy like he's in a competition. Every slam of his hips shoves Matt's cock so far down my throat, it's impossible for me to speak. I'm taking both of them deeper than I ever thought I could. I'm going to come, I know I am, I want to.

Before the pleasure erupts, Jace pulls out of me. I hate the immediate empty feeling, and I push back without thinking. I'm a greedy slut who needs more. My body is throbbing, and I'll do anything to come all over his cock.

"Focus," Jace says. "I haven't decided yet if you're coming today, and we're not done with you."

Fuuuuck. I want to protest, but Matt's cock in my mouth makes it impossible. Matt grips my hair, fucking my mouth vigorously while my brain keeps focusing on my ass and how much I want Jace's cock inside it.

Matt's voice is tight. "I want a turn with that pussy."

Jace must have agreed because Matt pulls out of my mouth. The men help me to my feet and then bend me over the desk. I don't get any warning before Matt's cock plunges into my pussy. I cry out from the pleasure. Matt is longer than Jace, and he's immediately knocking against a pleasurable spot deep inside me. Each thrust from Matt sends sparks of electricity to my toes, and I'm already close to coming.

"How does that pussy feel, Matt?"

Jace is talking like I'm not even here. Like I'm just an object. A toy for them to use. I groan at the thought and grip the edge of the desk harder. Each whack against my pussy is scraping my nipples against the wood and compounding my pleasure. I want to play with my clit and come for them.

"So warm and tight," Matt pants out as he jackhammers into me.

The friction in my pussy is more than I can take. Laying my head on the desk, I surrender to them and give up on coming. The desk smells of lemon cleaner, and it's almost as if I'm watching from above my body as the men use me. This is better than anything they've done to me before, and suddenly it doesn't matter if I don't come. I just want to make them happy.

I can feel my body tense as if I'm going to orgasm and then remember I'm not supposed to. Taking slow and steady breaths, I try to force my muscles to relax. I can't risk being a bad girl and them not fucking me. I've never felt like this before. I'm just a dirty slut craving cock.

"Uh oh, I think our fucktoy is going to come without permission."

Jace's voice holds a hint of amusement, and I cry out as Matt laughs. "You're right."

I'm doing everything I can to avoid coming, but it's not working. I can't stop it. I'm going to—

Matt pulls out of me an instant before the pleasure breaks and my pussy clenches around nothing. Nooooo. I mewl out in frustration. Oh holy shit. I'm so desperate to come. Why won't they let me come?

Matt presses his hand on my shoulder, so I can't stand up. "You know what I think?" His voice is teasing, and I can tell his question is directed towards Jace. "I think she's waiting for someone to fuck her ass."

I groan. Yes. God, yes, I want Jace to take my ass, but at this point, anyone's cock would do. I bet I'd come as soon as someone stretched me out. I want to orgasm like that, full and screaming.

"Too bad that she doesn't get to choose," Jace says. "Bring her here."

Matt takes a fistful of my hair and uses it to force me up. The pressure on my scalp is a painful pleasure, and I'm careful not to pull away from him. Matt makes me kneel again in front of Jace. I lick my lips as I stare at Jace's hard cock. The head is swollen and shiny, and I'm desperate to run my tongue over his veins.

Jace holds onto the base, aiming it at my mouth. "Suck it."

I open my mouth and glance over at my husband to make sure he's enjoying this. He's watching us intensely and rubbing his cock through his jeans. When he gives me a little smile and a nod, I engulf the tip of Jace's cock. My husband wants to see me be a slut, and I'm more than willing to play my part.

Jace barely needs to push me down, and I greedily suck on his cock. I can taste and smell myself on him, and I love how filthy it makes me feel. Licking my own wetness off someone's cock who isn't my husband is the right kind of dirty for me.

He groans as I deep throat him. "That's it. Just like that. Such a good little cocksucker."

Yes, I am. His praise makes me suck harder. This is as good as being a good girl. Maybe better. He's fucking my face steadily, and all I can do is kneel here and take it like a good cocksleeve.

"Now suck on Matt." His voice is tight, and I wish he had come, but I move over to Matt's cock like an obedient fucktoy.

I lick and clean my juices off Matt's cock, and the heady mixture makes my head spin. Jesus, this is so damn dirty and so fabulous. Jace kneels behind me and pulls my panties down to my knees. I'm so close to coming I really might explode as soon as he sinks into me.

Jace teases the head of his cock against the opening of my ass, and I groan. Oh god, what is he doing to me? He needs to just push it in. Do I have to beg?

I try to stay focused on Matt's cock in my mouth, but all I want to do is cry out and plead for Jace to fuck my ass.

Jace puts more pressure on my forbidden hole and growls, "Do you want my cock?"

"Yes." I struggle to get the words out around Matt's cock because right at that moment, Matt speeds up. His body is tensing, and I know he's close. I'm desperate to taste his cum, and I try to beg between thrusts in my throat. "Yes, please!"

"Tell us what you want," Jace demands, and I have to pull back from Matt for a moment to get the words out. "I want you to fuck my ass, Jace. Please? Fill me."

He presses harder, and I mewl from desire and slide my lips around Matt's cock again. Matt swears and pulls my head down firmly until my nose bumps against his pelvis. I'm so soaking wet I'm not sure Jace would even need lube to fuck my ass. He could just gather some moisture from my pussy and go for it. I'm such a slut, and I want to come with Jace slamming into my ass while Matt face fucks me.

Matt's thigh muscles quiver a second before he loses control. He comes violently, thick ropes of cum spurting down my throat as he keeps fucking my mouth and his entire body spasms. I lap it up as fast as I can, but there's so much that it's running down my chin.

As Matt sags back into the office chair, I grind on Jace's cock and try to think fast. "Please. You've been teasing me about using my ass since the day we met. I know you want it. Please? Fuck my ass."

"Greedy fucktoy," Jace says. "What do you say?"

It takes me a moment to realize that he's not talking to me. I look over my shoulder. Ian is sitting in a chair, stroking his cock through his jeans and watching these two guys turn me into a mindless fucktoy. He set all of this up for me, and the decision is up to my husband.

I could beg him, but I don't want to. The decision has to come from him. I'm a greedy, dirty slut. And I wait for him to choose.

After what seems like forever, Ian says, "No," and I moan loudly. Fuck.

Ian rubs his hardness under his jeans faster. "Her ass belongs to me. I'm not ready to share my toy yet."

When he calls me a toy, a warmth of love for my husband washes over me. I know he can't be a hard dom, which is why both of us enjoy what we do with Jace and Matt. Ian gets to see me turned into a desperate slut, and Jace gives me the harshness I crave. In a crazy way, Ian not sharing my ass today makes me feel loved and cared for.

When Jace hammers into my pussy, all other thoughts drain from my head. He drills into me, brutal and fast, and I'm crying out "Oh god," with every whack against my pussy. It's a glorious roughness, and I try to match his thrusts, forcing him to fuck me harder.

Jace's voice comes out in a puff between each thrust. "If you're a good girl and thank me afterwards, you can come."

My body lights up with pleasure, and I gasp as he continues. "But you better be quick. I'm about to fill this tight pussy, and then it's all over."

The thought of him filling me is all I need to come. My orgasm bursts through me, and stars twinkle along the corners of my vision as waves of ecstasy assault me. Jace fucks me through my orgasm, and I chant, "Thank you, thank you, thank you!" as the pleasure keeps going. My entire body shudders, and my pussy milks his cock, trying to get his cum.

He grunts, and right when I think I won and I'm about to get the payoff, he pulls out and yanks me up on my feet. He pushes me back onto his desk and removes my panties before he's between my thighs, lifting my knees with his forearms. I barely have time to get used to the new position before he's balls deep in my pussy again. The first thrust makes me scream as another orgasm rips through me like wildfire, sizzling all my nerve endings from my fingers to my toes.

He hooks one of my ankles up on his shoulder to free his hand and starts rubbing my clit. "After all that," he groans, "you think you're just going to get two?"

His hips slam into me, and the fingers on my clit speed up. My back arches as the pleasure is so intense I almost shatter to pieces. I'm filthy, this is filthy. Rapture tears through me without warning, and I cry out as I writhe from the pleasurable pain. It's almost too much.

"Fuuuuck," he grunts and explodes. His cum surges into me, thick and heavy. There's so much it's leaking out of me before he's even done. He fucks his cum into me as he spasms and jerks until he's done unloading. I'm full of cum from two different men and feeling completely satisfied.

I can barely think as the men move around me, kissing me and touching me softly. I'm not sure who is doing what, and I don't care. I feel amazing, and I'm floating in my happy place. The men clean me up and thank me for being such a good fucktoy. I'm mentally fuzzy, and all I can do is grin at them. When I'm tidy and dressed and clean, Ian takes my hand and leads me out to the car to head home.

CHAPTER 4

By the time we get back to the house, my brain is working again. I feel the best kind of filthy. That was a crazy experience, and I can't believe how much keeping me on the edge of coming would turn me into a desperate slut. Thinking about how I was willing to debase myself gets me wet and needy all over again. Fuck, that was hot.

We're barely inside the front door before Ian pushes me against the wall. Well, hello. I guess he's just as turned on as I am. Not that I'm surprised. He just watched me get used over and over again.

His mouth covers mine, and he lifts my tank top to play with my nipples. I whimper and groan, trying to push against him. I want him so much.

"You were a good little slut today," Ian says between kisses. "But I told you. Your ass is mine until I say someone else can have it."

"Oh god, please fuck me," I moan and beg. All those orgasms weren't enough, and I won't feel complete until Ian comes as well. "Please? I want you inside me."

Ian grins as he shoves my skirt and my panties down my hips. He helps me step out of them, then opens his jeans to pull his dick out. When he lifts my leg and hooks it around his waist, his cock slides into my pussy easily since I'm wet with Jace's cum still.

"Fuck, Erin. You're so hot."

My back is against the wall, and he slams against me for a moment before pulling out and dragging me to the living room. Jesus, the position changes are making my head spin. He sits on the couch and pulls me into his lap. I follow his lead and straddle him, sliding down onto his cock.

As I start to move and rock in his lap, he pulls my shirt off, then scoops my breasts out of my bra, playing with both nipples with his thumbs. I grind on him, feeling my body tense as he pumps up into me. Oh god, I think I'm going to come again.

I moan when he pulls on my nipples and says, "You were desperate to have it in the ass. Admit it."

"Yes. Fuck yes. It felt so good when you did it. I want more of it."

"Mmmm, nice. I'll give you more," he says as he tweaks my nipples roughly. His words sizzle my brain as I cry out with another orgasm. I drive down onto his cock as he slams up into me, fucking me through my orgasm. My pussy pulses and my body shakes as I ride him through the pleasure.

When the rapture dies down, he pushes me to my feet and bends me over the arm of the couch. Holy fuck, this is insane. I lay my cheek on the couch cushion while I hear his clothes rustle. The sound of plastic ripping and a pop top is the only warning I get before I feel the cool lube between my ass cheeks. Ooooh, yes!

"You were ready, just in case?" I giggle as his fingers stroke me, working gently into my ass to spread the lube around. The feeling is glorious, and my clit throbs from the pleasure.

"Of course," he says. Like it's the most obvious thing. "I wasn't sure if I was willing to share you yet, but I wanted to be prepared in case I was."

That's just like my man to think of everything. His fingers work more lube into my ass, and I groan, grinding back against him as he opens me up. When he's satisfied, he lines his cock up, and I feel the tip pressing against me. My body tightens in anticipation.

His hand strokes down my spine, calming me. "Breathe."

I do, but it's hard to relax when I want this so much. He pushes forward, and the burn is just as immense this time. But now I know how good it's going to feel in a moment—how dirty and delicious. It's easier to be calm and not tense up when you know how glorious everything is about to feel.

His head pops past the rim, and I groan at the sudden sense of being so beautifully full. I try to push back, to take him all, but he keeps my hips still. He sinks into me so slowly that it's driving me crazy after this afternoon. All I want is for him to fuck me, fill my ass up, and he's taking so long with it.

"Your ass is so tight," he says. "And it's mine. Remember?"

"Yes." How could I forget?

He keeps a slow, gentle pace until he's buried fully. I groan and shift, encouraging him to fuck me the way I want.

"So eager," he says, laughing a little. "You love my cock in your ass."

"I do," I mewl out. "So, fuck me already. Please?"

He keeps going slow, and it's killing me. I try to get leverage and shove my hips back to make him move faster, and he responds by giving me what I want as he drills into me.

"This hole is mine." His voice is strained. "Say it."

"It's yours! God, it's yours."

My body is singing as my breasts drag against the fabric of the couch with every slap of his hips against mine. I'm not sure I've ever felt this good.

"What's mine?" He growls, and I can tell he's feeling territorial.

"My ass." I'm close to screaming with pleasure. "My ass is yours."

"Rub your clit," he demands. "I want to feel you come while my cock is in your ass."

He doesn't have to tell me twice. I move a hand between my legs. My clit is sensitive and throbbing. It only takes a few strokes before I'm ready to explode.

"You're mine," he says again. "And I'll share my good fucktoy when I'm ready to."

That's all it takes. My husband's possessiveness sets off a chain reaction, and my body undulates as the pleasure overwhelms me. My entire body is clenching around his cock as I'm assaulted with sharp peaks of pleasure.

He keeps fucking me while the joy transcends me to a higher plane. The second I relax a little, he groans my name and shoots thick jets of cum into my ass, over and over.

He pulls his cock out and wraps me up into his arms. "You're so fucking sexy," he says, stroking my back. "I love you so much."

"God, Ian. I love you too." I mash my body against his, not wanting to break the connection.

We stay that way, just enjoying the moment, until we're both ready to clean up. We take a shower together and then cuddle up in bed, still naked. Ian pets my hair while our legs tangle together and I play footsie with him. My head is tucked under his chin, and I can't remember the last time I felt this relaxed.

"You're amazing," he says, kissing the top of my head.

I'm satisfied and feeling loved. I tighten my arms around him. "You're pretty great, too."

We're quiet for a moment, and I can't help but tease him. "Are you ever going to let Jace fuck my ass?" I make my voice all high and pouty, and he laughs.

"How about next time we get together with Jace and Matt?" He kisses the top of my head again. My heart starts to pound, and even as tired and sated as I am, my pussy gives a little whimper of pleasure as he continues. "Next time, I'll share your ass."

I give his chest tons of little kisses. "You, sir, have just earned yourself a private pole dance."

He chuckles, and I feel it rumble through his chest as I melt into him. I really am the luckiest slut in the world, and I can't wait to see Jace and Matt again.

The End

THE SLUTTY WIFE'S DESIRES

HOTWIFE EXPLORATION 5

LACEY CROSS

Chapter 1

I'm nestled in bed, cocooned under the blankets, when Ian joins me after brushing his teeth. This is my favorite time of the day. I get to snuggle with my man and enjoy a few minutes of connection, even on our busiest days.

I rest my head on his chest as he caresses my back. My mind begins to wander, reflecting on how much my life has changed since embracing my desires and becoming a hotwife. It's been an exhilarating journey of self-discovery. Who knew I would be so hot for backdoor action? Not this girl.

The experiences have been intoxicating—all orchestrated by my wonderful husband. That first day when I offered myself to Jace and Matt at the veterinarian clinic, I had no idea that becoming a hotwife would strengthen my marriage...but it has. Having a husband who loves watching me with other guys is pretty fucking fabulous. This really is the life.

I sigh contentedly and snuggle closer into the warmth of his chest, lightly tracing my fingertips around his nipples.

"Babe?" I whisper softly. "I've been thinking a lot lately...about us. About this whole hotwife thing."

"Mmm, is that so?" Ian's voice is a deep, soothing rumble as he gently strokes my back.

I tilt my head to look up at him and grin. "Is it weird that I feel closer to you after fucking other men?"

Ian laughs. "That's because you're my sexy slut who likes being naughty."

A flush of pleasure warms me. "You're really okay with it, though? You don't want to stop?"

"Sweetheart, I'm more than okay with it," he assures me, his eyes glimmering with mischief. "In fact...I may have a little surprise planned for this weekend."

My heart skips a beat, and I want to squeal in excitement. Is he finally going to let Jace fuck my ass? I try to play it cool and keep my voice flirty as I walk my fingers up his chest. "A surprise? What is it? You know I hate waiting."

Ian chuckles, capturing my hand and bringing it to his lips for a kiss. "Sorry, love. You'll have to wait and see. But trust me, you're going to love it," he promises with a wink.

I pout dramatically, giving him my best puppy dog eyes. "Oooh, you're such a tease! Not even a tiny hint?"

"Nope!" He grins, tapping my nose playfully. "But have I ever disappointed you before?"

"No, your surprises are always amazing," I admit, snuggling closer. "You just get me. I suppose I can wait."

Just because I'm waiting doesn't mean I won't fantasize. It's going to be a week of raunchy daydreams.

Ian tenderly cups my face, his expression adoring as he gazes into my eyes. "I'm the luckiest man alive."

"Mmm, and don't you forget it, mister." I give him a slow, sensual kiss, savoring his familiar taste and the scrape of his stubble against my skin.

Ian pulls me on top of him, and my knees rest on the mattress on either side of him. I can feel his hard cock through his pajama pants as I fit my pussy against it and gently rotate my hips. I guess we're not going straight to sleep.

His fingers trace circles on my lower back before they trail down to cradle my butt. "I love your ass," he murmurs. "And it's all mine."

His words make me squirm in delight. He recently installed a stripper pole in the spare room for me because he knew I wanted one, and I've been taking pole dancing lessons. My ass is firmer than it's been in years, and even I enjoy admiring myself in the mirror.

He grips my buttcheeks and forces me to rock against his hardness. A pleasurable tingle swirls in my core as I try to be cute. "But maybe you want to share my ass sometime...like this weekend?"

He's been teasing me about letting Jace, our cat's veterinarian, fuck my ass, and I'm really, really hoping that's the surprise this weekend. I've had several hotwife encounters, but Jace and his technician Matt are my two main play partners.

"Maybe," he says with a grin as he moves a hand between us. I lift up slightly so he can pull his cock from his pajamas. He pushes aside my panties, and I sigh in pleasure as he slides inside me.

"Hmm, someone is nice and wet at the thought of getting their ass used," he groans.

"It's all for you, babe," I whisper as I slowly ride him.

He and I both know that the thought of Jace fucking my ass makes me instantly wet, but this is the game we play. He teases me about that hole being only his, and I try to pretend I don't want anyone else.

I kiss him again, our tongues swirling together as I imagine Ian really letting Jace fuck my ass. I've only ever done anal with Ian and I'm new to it, but I'm quickly turning into a slut at the thought of Jace's thick cock sliding inside my ass.

Keeping my movements slow, it's not long before Ian has his hands on my hips and tries to make me grind faster against his cock. When I don't speed up, he rolls us over until he's on top.

I moan and wrap my legs around him as he fucks me hard. He pants out, "If you want Jace to fuck your ass, you're going to have to beg for it."

His words turn me on even more. I whimper and writhe, desperately grinding against him as he keeps plunging deep into my pussy. God, I love this man. He gets me so fucking hot.

We move together as I shamelessly plead. "Please, baby. Please! I want Jace to fuck my ass!"

He looks pleased, and he rewards me by lifting my legs higher and fucking me harder. I continue to chant, "Please," while he pumps into me and my eyes roll back in my head. Fuck, yes! I think I'm going to get what I want.

Ian kisses me again as we move faster. I whine against his lips in desperation. My pussy aches, clenching tightly around him, as the pleasure builds.

His voice is thick with lust as he asks, "You want another man to use my hole?"

I nod frantically as the bliss spirals in my core. I'm going to come any moment. "I need it. Please. I want him to fill my ass with his cum."

Hearing my own filthy words come out of my mouth almost tips me over the edge.

"That's my dirty slut," Ian groans.

When he gives a sharp thrust, I cry out and explode with pleasure. Delight rushes through me, and my pussy clamps around him. Ian jackhammers against me and erupts, filling me with his seed.

I arch my back and sob in rapture, gasping from aftershocks of pleasure. I tremble as I come down from the euphoric high. Holy shit, that was intense.

When he collapses beside me, I cuddle up against him, sighing contentedly. Ian kisses me softly, and when he speaks, the tone of his voice is amused. "I guess you really want it. We'll see how I feel on Saturday."

I want to protest that I did a good enough job begging that I deserve my reward, but I'm too content. "Okay, love. We'll just see on Saturday."

The workout has exhausted me, and within a few minutes, I'm out like a light, dreaming about being filled up by Jace and having every hole used.

CHAPTER 2

Ian is awake and out of bed before me on Saturday, and I'm so excited I practically dance into the kitchen. He's leaning against the counter, sipping his coffee, looking unfairly handsome in a simple t-shirt and jeans.

I greet him in a sing-song voice. "Good morning, my love."

He raises his eyebrows at me while he takes a sip of his coffee. After I pour myself a cup, I sidle up to him with a mischievous grin. "So...about tonight. Can't you give me a little clue? A tiny hint about what you've got planned?"

Ian chuckles, setting down his mug and looping an arm around my waist. "Well, well, someone's certainly eager. But my insatiable wife is going to have to wait. Patience is a virtue, remember? All will be revealed in due time."

I pout playfully, batting my lashes. "But I'm no good at patience, you know that. Come on, babe. Just a little morsel to tide me over? I can make it worth your time?"

I run a hand over his cock and feel it twitch underneath his jeans. When he pulls away, I pout again while he grins affectionately.

"Nice try, but I'm not spoiling the surprise. Trust me, you'll like it."

My mind races with possibilities. Jace and Matt must be coming over—and if Ian is really considering letting someone else fuck my ass, it would be Jace.

Ian finishes his coffee and sets his mug in the sink before kissing my forehead. "All right, I need to run an errand. There's something I need to get for tonight's festivities."

"Ooh, intriguing." I tilt my face up for a proper kiss goodbye. "Hurry back to me. I'll just be here, you know, slowly dying of curiosity."

"So dramatic," he teases, smacking my ass playfully as he heads out. "Don't get into too much trouble while I'm gone."

The second the door closes behind him, I bolt for our bedroom, tearing through my closet with single-minded determination. What to wear, what to wear...I need an ensemble that screams "irresistible sex goddess."

When I can't decide, I call my best friend, Sasha.

She answers with a yawn. "Yo, what's up?"

Sasha grew up only being allowed to watch 80s re-runs, and the way she talks always makes me smile.

"Hey, wake up. I need your help. Ian invited a guy over tonight to fuck me, and I need to know what to wear."

Or at least I assume he invited someone over...he better have.

She groans, and it sounds like she's pulling covers over her head. "You woke me up to brag about all the cock you're getting when you know my husband won't share?"

She likes to grumble good-naturedly about my sexcapades, but she also loves hearing about them.

"Fine, I won't tell you the details..."

That makes her giggle. "Now, now...don't be hasty. What're the options?"

I describe five outfits, but before she can tell me her opinion, she swears. "Shit, I gotta go. I just heard the garage door open, and I've got to help unload groceries."

I laugh. "Fine, I'll figure this out myself!"

She hangs up with a, "Love ya!" and I survey my choices again. Well shit, she was no help.

I mull over what I'm going to wear as I think about Sasha's situation and how lucky I am. Ian really is the best husband.

Sighing, I look at my lingerie again and give up. I'll take a shower and think about it.

By the time Ian returns, shopping bag in hand, I'm fresh from the shower and wrapped in a towel, agonizing over two different sets of lingerie.

He clears his throat from the doorway. "I see you've been productive," he observes wryly.

I stick my tongue out at him. "Hush, just trust the process. Wait, what's in the bag? Gimme!"

"So demanding, too." Ian shakes his head with a smile, handing over the goods. "I picked up a little something for you. For tonight."

I reach into the bag eagerly, pulling out a stunning pink negligee. It's sheer lace, and I can tell that the low cut is going to give everyone a tantalizing view while still leaving something to the imagination. It's sinfully sexy and utterly perfect.

"Ohhh..." I breathe, running my fingers over the delicate fabric. "It's beautiful."

He looks pleased with himself. "I'm glad you like it. But I want to tell you the plan for tonight because you have a choice to make."

"Oh?" Hopefully, this plan includes whether I want Jace's cock in my ass. The answer is 'yes.'

Ian takes my hand, rubbing his thumb over my knuckles soothingly. "Mack is coming over."

"Mack?" Surprise floods through me, followed by a pleasurable thrill. I haven't seen Mack since that afternoon at his place when Ian watched him ravish me in the backyard. God, that was fun. I can't be unhappy about getting another shot at his monster cock, even if it means I don't get Jace in my ass tonight.

"I think we could get up to some sexy trouble together."

Ian pulls me against him and gives me a quick kiss. "Perfect. Mack mentioned he'd love to see you twirling around the stripper pole if you're up for it..."

The idea sends liquid heat pulsing through my veins. "I think I can manage that," I reply coyly. "You know how much I love putting on a show."

Ian's eyes darken with desire. "Mmm, that I do. Have I mentioned lately how incredible you are? How much I adore you?"

"You're not so bad yourself, stud." I wink, looping my arms around his neck. "But you know what they say—show, don't tell."

He growls playfully, pulling me flush against him. "Oh, I'll show you all right. Later. When I have you all to myself again."

I shiver at the promise in his voice. "Can't wait, but I want at least four orgasms tonight, so if Mack doesn't deliver, you better be prepared to bring your A game."

He laughs. "Deal."

I reluctantly disentangle myself and shoo him out so I can finish getting ready. I put my hair in a high ponytail so it doesn't get messy when I dance, and as I shimmy into the negligee, I study my reflection in the mirror. The lace clings to my curves, the sheerness hinting at the bare skin beneath. I look daring. Sensual. Desirable. Like a woman ready to embrace whatever happens.

Mack isn't Jace and Matt, but variety is the spice of life, right? And novelty can be its own aphrodisiac. My ass might not get fucked tonight, but that just means I'll want it all the more when it actually happens. Besides, I'll be too busy trying to stuff Mack's enormous cock in me to even think about Jace.

Drawing in a deep, steadying breath, I smooth the negligee over my hips and psych myself up to shake my booty for the love of my life and his best friend from college. Maybe Ian will get so horny he'll want me to suck on him while Mack fucks me. Mmm, I love being spit roasted. A girl can dream, right?

CHAPTER 3

The doorbell's chime echoes through the house, sending my heart leaping into my throat. Mack's here! This is really happening.

Ian pops his head into the bedroom, his expression a mix of excitement and reassurance. "Stay put, love. I'll get the door and text you when we're ready for your grand entrance."

I nod, and right as he turns to leave, he pauses. "You look absolutely incredible." His eyes shine with adoration and undisguised hunger. When the doorbell rings again, he winks. "See you soon, baby."

He leaves, and I'm suddenly a bundle of nervous energy. Ian converted our spare room into a sensual playground for us, with a pole and two couches, plus mood lighting and a sound system. I've only danced for a few people other than Ian, and I'm always worried I'll look awkward and unsexy. Logically, I know the feeling is unfounded because I'm hot—becoming a hotwife has given me a fuckton more confidence. Plus, Ian isn't going to invite anyone over who isn't enthusiastic about watching me dance. But I still get a tiny bit of stage fright every time.

I pace my bedroom, checking my hair, my makeup, the drape of the negligee for the hundredth time. The waiting is always the hardest part, anticipation building until I'm ready to crawl out of my skin.

After what feels like an eternity, my phone dings with a text from Ian.

It's time.

Slipping on a pair of black high heels, I hurry down the hall, pausing outside the spare room. The music mix that I made for dancing is on, and I can hear it through the door. It helps to calm my nerves as memories rush back, snapshots of the first time I danced for an audience—Ian, Jace, and Matt, their appreciative eyes fueling my confidence, my desire...

I'm ready.

I open the door and freeze, mouth falling open in shock. Four pairs of eyes meet mine—Ian, Mack, Jace, and Matt. They're all here. All of them, wearing matching grins.

Surprise gives way to pure, incandescent delight. They came. They all came for me. I almost giggle at the thought—well, they haven't all come yet. But hopefully soon.

As if on cue, the music changes to my favorite song, and the beat gives me an electrical charge. These guys are here to fuck me. I feel powerful. A goddess in the flesh.

Hips swaying, I step into the room, letting the door fall shut behind me. "Hi, guys."

I lock eyes with Ian, his face glowing with fierce pride and unconditional love. It fills me up, gives me the strength to embrace the wild, wanton side of myself.

Looking at each man in turn, I give them all a smile, saving Jace for last. When I meet his gaze, a shiver of longing tingles along my spine. Oh, the things he could do to me...the things I hope he does to me tonight...

The guys all murmur hello, and I can tell they're already entranced. Jace's deep, velvety voice stands out when he says, "Are you going to be a good girl and dance for us?"

His 'good girl' fries my brain, and it's difficult to answer. My entire body tingles, and I sound breathy when I finally say, "Yes."

With the room feeling like it's spinning, I stand in front of the stripper pole and let the music pulse through me. Closing my eyes, I start slowly, my arms above my head as my hips undulate to the music. The beat vibrates through my body, guiding my movements as I lose myself to the rhythm. My fingers splay across my stomach, moving up to my breasts. Even though my eyes are closed, I know everyone is watching me...wanting me. I can feel myself getting wetter, and I want to give these men everything.

I dance for my men—for the one who holds my heart and the ones who set my body on fire. There's no thought beyond this moment and the sensual glide of the silk on my skin and the heat of their gazes following my every move.

Each appreciative murmur spurs me on, every low groan igniting me. I've never felt sexier, more powerful, more alive. I'm embracing the moment, and anything feels possible tonight.

As I dance, the negligee gives them brief peeks of the skin underneath. I'm an inferno of lust as time becomes meaningless. The world narrows to the sway of my hips, the arch of my back, the simmering hunger building in the room.

I hook a leg around the gleaming pole, letting my head fall back. This is my element, where I'm utterly confident, completely free—a goddess of desire, reveling in her own allure.

When the song ends and a slower one starts, I pause and look at the men. My chest heaves, and I can feel my skin flush with arousal. I'm ready for someone to fuck me.

Ian and Jace are on one couch, and Matt and Mack are on the other. I focus on Ian, swaying my hips as I move to stand in front of him. I'm desperate for someone to touch me, to quench this thirst I have for all their cocks.

Ian leans forward, sliding a finger under a strap of the negligee and drawing it off my shoulder slowly. He drops it and moves the other off. The front dips down, and my nipples peek out. He slips the straps over my arms, and the garment falls to the floor to puddle at my feet. All I'm wearing now are my panties and the high heels.

To the side of me, I hear someone suck in a breath. I tilt my head towards Matt and Mack, and both are staring at me with unbridled lust. I feel it to my very core.

Ian's voice is rough when he speaks. "Who's going to take her first?"

Jace stands, leaving no doubts about his intention to make the first move. My heart races as I feel the desire humming between Jace and me as Jace steps closer.

"You look so tempting," Jace murmurs, his voice low and dangerous. His fingers trail along my jaw, tilting my head up to meet his eyes.

I glance over at Ian and see the raw desire burning in his eyes. He nods slightly, silently giving me permission to surrender to Jace.

Jace's lips clash with mine, his tongue delving into my mouth, and I feel my insides melt. I'm ready to wrap my legs around him and beg him to fuck me right when he breaks off the kiss.

"Are you ready to be a dirty little slut and take all our cocks?"

"Yes."

Mmmm, hell yes, I am.

Jace pushes me to my knees before taking his cock out of his jeans. It's thick and long, and I lick my lips as I remember how he feels in my mouth. I lean towards him and part my lips, looking at him in case he stops me. He doesn't.

His shaft slides into my mouth, and I moan in pleasure as I taste his pre-cum. Knowing the other guys are watching me give Jace a blowjob makes me want to do a good job of it, so they wish it was them—especially my husband. I trail my tongue along his shaft, savoring the taste of him as my tongue explores the contours of his thick veins.

As I bob my head up and down, he slides his hands around the back of my head to control my movements. He pulls me closer as he thrusts into my mouth. The base of his cock smacks against my chin, coating it with a sheen of spit as I deep throat him. It's messy and I'm getting saliva around my mouth, but I don't care. I want to see if I can make him come.

I relax my throat as he face fucks me, allowing him to speed up his thrusts. The more aggressive he becomes, the wetter my pussy gets. The next time I take him in fully, he holds me there, my throat working around his shaft. He groans and pulls out right before he comes.

Jesus, this is hot. I wanted to taste him, but I love feeling like a toy that the men can use however they want, so letting him decide what happens makes this better.

Jace pulls me up to my feet, his lips crashing against mine in a bruising kiss. He plunders my mouth, and I wish his cock was inside me while he was doing it. I don't know what it is about Jace, but everything about him just does it for me. I lucked out when I decided to see if he offered extra services that day weeks ago at the veterinarian clinic. If I had been looking for a regular play partner, I couldn't have found someone who turns me on more. He seems to know exactly what I like.

When he finally pulls away, I'm panting, my lips swollen and wet. He cups my chin and brushes his thumb across my lips. I want to suck on his thumb, but his next words stop me.

"You're such a good little cocksucker. I think it's time you shared that pretty mouth of yours with the others."

Oooh, I couldn't agree more. When he presses on my shoulders, I sink to the floor again and look up at him, waiting for instructions.

"Crawl over to Matt and Mack," Jace commands. "And suck on their cocks too. Show them how much of a cock-greedy slut you are."

I practically purr as I glance over and see Matt and Mack still sitting on the couch. But now they both have their cocks out. Yeah, this is dirty. I can't wait to get my hands and mouth on them.

Slowly, I crawl across the floor, wiggling my ass for Jace and Ian's enjoyment. I want them both thinking of Jace sinking his thick cock into my ass. If that doesn't happen tonight, I better get lots of orgasms to make up for it.

When I reach the couch, I pause and sit up on my knees. I'm uncertain who I'm supposed to suck on first.

Mack chuckles as if he can see my uncertainty. He holds the base of his thick shaft and motions me over. "Well, don't just stare, slut. Get to work."

Mmm, guess it's Mack first. I crawl between his legs and hesitate as I wrap my hand around the base of his monstrous cock. Mack has the biggest cock in the room, and the one time I fucked him, I thought he was splitting me in two. How am I going to get that all in my mouth?

Fuck it, I'm going to try. I lean in, wrapping my lips around the head of his cock and relaxing my jaw so I can take as much as I can into my mouth. It doesn't seem like I've got much in there, but Mack groans so I can tell he's enjoying it. To give him more pleasure, I make the blow job super messy. Saliva drips down his shaft, and I use my hands to massage the half of his shaft that won't fit in my mouth. Sucking on a guy who is too big to fully take inside my mouth gives me a nice slutty feeling, like I'm just a mouth hole for this guy to use.

Movement next to us makes me peek over at Matt. He's stroking his cock while he watches me try my best on the enormous shaft in my mouth.

"Switch," Jace's voice rings out.

When I pull up off of Mack's cock, I give him my best cutesy smile. "Sorry, that's all you get. Duty calls."

He grins and rubs the saliva off my lips with his thumb. "I'll get more of what I want later."

Oh, I bet he will. Crawling between Matt's legs, I turn my attention to him. I've given Matt multiple blowjobs over the last few months, so I know what he likes. I lick and kiss up and down his length before opening my mouth wide to take him in. This is the third cock in my mouth tonight, and I love how each guy has a unique taste and feel against my tongue.

Matt has always been an enthusiastic lover, and as I suck on him, I enjoy his moans and harsh breathing. He doesn't seem to be in any danger of coming, so I throw myself on his cock, hollowing my cheeks and applying suction. Even though I'm sucking on him, my arousal builds with each passing moment, until I'm a trembling, needy mess, aching to be used.

Suddenly, Ian's voice breaks through the haze. "Erin, my love, I think it's time we take this to the bedroom." His words are laced with a mixture of tenderness and arousal.

I reluctantly pop up off of Matt's cock and give him a cheeky grin. Matt's eyes are dark with lust, and I get a thrill from knowing I did a good job. I bet I could have made Matt come if I had more time.

Ian moves to me and gently helps me to my feet. His strong arms steady me as my head spins.

"Easy there, love," he murmurs, guiding me towards the bedroom. I lean into him, my body trembling with lust. I need a cock inside me—maybe two.

CHAPTER 4

The guys follow us into the bedroom. The room is dimly lit, casting a warm, sensual glow over everything. Ian leads me to the bed and gently lowers me down. I kick off my high heels, and as I sit on the edge, I watch Jace carry in a chair. He positions it facing the bed. When Ian sits down in it, I get a jolt of pleasure. Well, that's nice and dirty. He's getting comfortable to watch three guys fuck me.

Jace moves in front of me and brushes a stray lock of hair from my face. "Erin," he says softly, "do you trust me?"

I don't hesitate before answering. "Yes, I trust you."

And I do trust him. I've fucked Jace and Matt multiple times, and even when they're being rough, they are careful with me. It's what makes them such good play partners.

The sound of the drawer of the nightstand opening makes me glance over. Ian gets something out and hands it to Jace. It's a silk blindfold that I've never seen before. Huh, looks like someone bought more than just lingerie for tonight.

Jace holds it up in front of me. "You good with this?"

"Oh god, please."

Like I'm going to say no to being blindfolded and ravished by multiple men? This is one of my top five fantasies, and I've told Ian that before.

This isn't a coincidence, and it's another example of my incredible husband making sure I get my fantasies fulfilled.

Jace places the blindfold over my eyes, plunging me into darkness while he secures it in the back of my head. The loss of my sight heightens my other senses, and I become acutely aware of the sounds and sensations around me. I can hear the men breathing, the rustle of fabric as someone undresses, and the creak of the chair as Ian shifts his weight. My skin tingles with anticipation, every nerve ending alive.

Suddenly, I feel lips on mine, and I know it's Jace. He kisses me deeply as his hands caress my body, igniting sparks of pleasure wherever he touches. I melt into his embrace, my body responding to his every move.

I feel the bed dip as someone else joins us. This person's hands are strong and confident, and from the feel of him, I'd guess it's Mack. He explores my curves, and whenever he hits a ticklish spot, I gasp in pleasure.

The sensations are overwhelming, and I feel myself being pulled more and more deeply into the erotic haze. I'm completely at the mercy of these two men, and the thought thrills me to my core.

They push me down until I'm lying on my back. My heart races as I realize I don't know what to expect since I can't see them. Hands roam over my body, and it's three sets. I shiver as unknown fingers trail down my sides, electrifying every nerve in my body.

One man grabs my thighs, gently parting them. I feel exposed and vulnerable, but the trust I have in these men keeps me pliant. Another man settles between my legs, his breath hot against my pussy. Holy hell, someone is holding me open for someone else? That's filthy and hot.

I moan as his tongue darts out, teasing my clit and tasting me. For some reason, I expected them to go straight to the fucking. I didn't imagine anyone would go down on me. Not knowing who it is makes this dirtier, and I can feel my orgasm building. My toes curl and I arch my back as the pleasure threatens to consume me.

Before I come, another man captures my mouth in a searing kiss that steals my breath away. I think that's Mack? The sensations are overwhelming, yet I have no idea which man is doing what to me. My mind is lost in a haze of lust, my body alive with sensation. Their skilled hands and tongues have me teetering on the edge while I rock my hips against the mouth on my pussy.

"Ohhhh god," I moan, almost feeling crazed by how amazing this all is.

Just as I think I can't take anymore, they switch places. A new guy is between my legs, this one licking and sucking harder. Jesus, maybe that's Matt? He seems less skilled and more eager, and my pussy loves the attention. When the person slides a finger inside me, the digit seems thicker than I remember Matt's being, and I give up on trying to figure out who is doing what.

I surrender myself completely to them as my inhibitions are stripped away. A third guy takes his turn at my pussy, and this time, I can't hold back my orgasm.

I cry out as my muscles spasm and pleasure floods my system. I buck my hips as ripples of ecstasy turn my mind to mush. When I come down, I'm panting, my body tingling.

"That's the first one," Ian says from his chair, and I giggle, remembering how I told him I wanted four orgasms. With three other men, plus Ian, somehow, I don't think this is going to be a problem.

Someone lies next to me on the bed. It's Matt who speaks. "Get on top of me."

My heart races as I carefully straddle his hips, his firm hands helping me. Slowly, I lower myself down, gasping as his cock slides into me. The sensation is exquisite, made even more intense by the blindfold.

With my sight blocked and my other senses heightened, I can feel every inch of him filling me. It's a delicious friction as I begin to move my hips. The scent of our mingled arousal fills the air, spurring me on. Matt's hands grip my waist, helping me find a steady rhythm. Each time I sink down onto him, a shudder of pleasure ripples through me.

"That's it," Matt groans, his voice husky from desire. "Ride me."

I lose myself in the sensations as his cock massages me every time I sink down on it. I can hear the wet sound of us slapping together as I ride him. It's obscene and wonderful. Waves of ecstasy build within me, my movements becoming more frantic as I chase the pleasure.

Matt meets each of my thrusts, driving himself deeper. The tension coils more and more tightly until finally, it shatters. My body convulses around him, stars bursting behind the darkness of the blindfold.

"That's two," Ian says, and I can't do anything but moan.

I hear the telltale sound of the lube bottle opening, and I grind against Matt's cock in anticipation. Oh god, I know what this means. It means Ian is the most wonderful husband on the planet and he's agreed to share my ass.

A strong hand presses firmly between my shoulder blades, pushing my upper body down towards Matt. I'm completely exposed, and slick fingers glide along my ass crack, circling my puckered hole. I moan softly, my body trembling with arousal. The fingers probe gently, working the lube in until I feel completely slick and open. Just the thought of what's about to happen makes my pussy clench around Matt's shaft.

Suddenly, I feel the blunt head of a cock pressing against my well-lubricated opening. My breath catches as it slowly sinks inside, stretching me deliciously. I bite my lip, trying to stay still as, inch by inch, I'm filled.

A groan rumbles from behind me, and powerful hands grasp my hips, pulling me back onto the thick shaft. I cry out, the sensation of two cocks in me at once bordering on too much, yet it's somehow perfect. Based on the size of the cock, I'm assuming it's Jace behind me. He begins to move, withdrawing almost completely before driving back in.

Each thrust into my ass forces me down onto Matt's cock. The dual pleasure makes me moan continuously. I can feel every inch of them massaging me, and it feels like I'm going to explode from pleasure.

The pace builds, each thrust into my ass harder and deeper than the last.

I'm lost in a haze of ecstasy. I'm just a mindless doll being used by both these men. All I can do is rock back to meet every punishing plunge.

"Fuck, you feel amazing," a deep voice rasps, and I know I was right. It's Jace fucking my ass. Finally.

Just knowing it really is him almost tips me over the edge. The guys have been teasing me for weeks about Jace fucking my ass, and being double stuffed is even better than I imagined. I'm going to remember this night forever.

Jace hammers into me relentlessly, and the pleasure builds. I'm like a toy being wound up more and more tightly until I'm trembling, on the edge of release. When Matt plays with my nipples and pulls on them, the sensation is too much. I cry out as another orgasm hits, my inner muscles clenching around him as waves of pleasure crash through me.

I'm chanting, "Fuck, fuck, fuck," as the bliss spikes and recedes and the men continue to fuck me.

When the pleasure finally dies down, I collapse, boneless, into Matt. Jace withdraws slowly, a soft whimper escaping my lips at the loss. I feel so wonderfully full, so thoroughly used.

A hand caresses my flushed cheek.

"Good girl," Jace murmurs. "But we're not done with you."

My husband's voice sounds thick with lust when he says, "Three."

This time my head is too mushy to giggle. When Jace slides his cock back into my ass, I moan loudly from pleasure. Holy fuck, this is crazy in the best of ways.

I'm overwhelmed with sensations, my body still trembling from the orgasm. The bed dips as someone settles next to me—I'm assuming Mack. His strong hand guides my head towards his cock. I open my mouth eagerly, thrilling at the idea of becoming the ultimate slut servicing three men at once.

Mack's cock brushes against my lips, and I part them, letting him slide into my waiting mouth. Due to his massive size, I can't take him all down and he doesn't try to force it. The familiar salty taste of him sends a shiver through me. As I begin to suck and lick, I hear Ian's voice, low and approving. He better be loving this show. It's not often his wife is going to get three holes stuffed at once.

The thought sends a fresh wave of arousal through me. My body feels like it's on fire, hyper-sensitive to every touch and sensation. Jace and Matt continue to fuck me, their thrusts deep and relentless. I moan around Mack's cock, the vibrations eliciting a groan from him.

I'm completely surrounded, utterly possessed by the men. Every inch of me is filled, used, claimed. I've never felt so wanton, so thoroughly debased. And yet, I've never felt sexier.

The pleasure builds until I'm trembling on the edge of ecstasy once more. I redouble my efforts, sucking Mack harder and rocking between the two cocks in me.

"That's it, slut. Take it all," Mack growls, his fingers tangling in my hair.

I'm drowning in the sensation of being so thoroughly and deliciously stuffed. I hope this moment lasts forever, that I can stay like this, a writhing, moaning mess of pure bliss.

Jace's tone is dominant. "You're such a dirty slut, taking all of us at once." His words send a shiver of pleasure down my spine. "But you love it, don't you? You love having all your holes filled."

My mouth is too full to respond, so all I can do is mumble around Mack's cock. Mack groans, "Fuck, yeah, that's it, baby. Suck me harder."

Jace's grasp on my hips tightens as he drives into me. "Look at you, getting off on being our shared slut. You were born for this, weren't you?"

His words send a buzz through my body. Having all these men inside me while Ian watches does feel right, like this is what I was meant to do. I know it sounds crazy, but right now my brain is foggy from so much pleasure, I want everything. Just thinking about how much of a slut I am pushes me closer to another orgasm.

"You're gonna come for us, aren't you?" Jace growls. "Because good girls come when they're told to."

Mmm, I am a good girl, and I enjoy doing what I'm told. I can't tell him that, because of Mack's cock stuffed in my mouth, so I try to show him I'm a good girl by rotating my hips faster.

Jace demands, "Come for us."

His words, combined with the pounding rhythms of their thrusts, sky-rocket me into another plane of existence. My orgasm rips through me, wave after wave of blinding ecstasy. I cry out around Mack's cock, my body convulsing as I shatter into a million pieces.

"Four," Ian calls out, his voice strained with his own arousal as he watches the depraved scene unfold before him.

Mack groans, "Fuck, her mouth feels so good, I'm not going to last much longer."

Jace yanks on my hair, pulling me off Mack's cock, as he asks, "Are you a greedy cum slut who wants us to come in all your holes?"

I whimper at the thought, my pussy clenching in anticipation. "Yes, please," I say breathlessly. "Please fill me up."

Jace chuckles darkly. "Then beg for it. Beg us to use you and fill you so full of cum that it's dripping out of you."

I don't hesitate, the words spilling from me in a desperate plea. "Please, please come inside me. I want all your cum. I want it all over me, in every hole. Use me, own me, make me come over and over again. I'll do anything, just please don't stop. Need all the cum!"

I'm trembling with desire, my body aching to be filled by them. Jace's grip on my hair tightens as he laughs. "What do you think, Ian? Does your slut wife want it enough?"

Oh god, don't ask him. He might say no!

"Oh, I think she wants it more than anything," he says, his voice low and ragged. "Look at her, begging for it. She deserves to get every last drop."

My heart races at Ian's words, relief washing over me. Jace pushes my head back towards Mack's cock, and Mack guides his shaft between my lips.

Jace growls, "You heard your husband, slut. You're about to get exactly what you asked for."

My body is on fire as the three men ravage me. Jace's thick shaft pulses deep in my ass, stretching and filling me. Matt's cock strokes my sensitive inner walls, hitting all the right spots. And Mack's huge member fills my mouth, hitting the back of my throat with each thrust.

The sensations are overwhelming, and with the blindfold on, everything is surreal. I moan around Mack's shaft, and he grips the back of my head, holding me in place as he fucks my mouth.

Jace's fingers dig into my hips, his pace becoming erratic as he chases his climax. "Fuck, you feel so good," he growls. "Taking all of us like the greedy slut you are."

Matt leans forward, his breath hot on my ear. "That's it, baby. Squeeze my cock with that needy little pussy." He reaches down to furiously rub my swollen clit, sending me spiraling towards the edge.

The men are relentless as they pound into me. When another orgasm hits me, my body convulses around the thrusting cocks. Wave after wave of mind-numbing pleasure washes over me, leaving me trembling and breathless.

Through the fog of my climax, I vaguely hear my husband's voice. His tone is a mix of pride and awe. "Five."

The ecstasy seems to go on forever as the men continue pounding into me. I feel completely overwhelmed by the sensations, my body quivering with pleasure.

The combination of these three powerful men using my body is beyond anything I could have imagined. I'm drowning in a sea of carnal bliss, my senses overloaded with the sounds and smells of our depraved union.

Suddenly, the men let out groans, and their bodies stiffen. I feel Matt come first as he coats my pussy walls. Then Jace spasms and pumps his hot seed deep into my ass while Mack floods my mouth with his thick, salty release.

My mind is blown, and another massive orgasm hits me. I can feel their cum spurting and pulsing, coating my insides. I swallow Mack's load greedily as the other two men finish emptying themselves into my needy holes.

It feels like it goes on forever, wave after wave of pure bliss. I'm completely lost in a haze of satisfaction. When they finally finish, I'm trembling, my body buzzing with the aftershocks of the most intense orgasm of my life.

Slowly, the men pull out of me, and Jace gently helps me lie down. He removes my blindfold, and I blink, adjusting to the soft light. Jace looks down at me, his eyes filled with satisfaction.

"Are you okay?" he asks softly.

I nod, still trying to catch my breath. "Yes, I'm...I'm amazing," I manage to get out, my voice barely above a whisper.

Jace smiles, and I feel a deep sense of contentment wash over me. I got what I wanted. My husband finally shared my ass with Jace.

I close my eyes and mentally drift, allowing the afterglow to envelop me. I can hear the men moving around, getting dressed to leave.

Ian comes over to me and caresses my cheek. When I open my eyes, he says, "I'm going to show them out. I'll be back."

There's a tenderness in his eyes, but also something else...my husband needs me.

"Okay, love. I'll be here." I giggle at my words. Where else would I be?

CHAPTER 5

I'm not sure how long Ian is gone, but when he comes back, he's naked. The bed dips as he climbs in beside me. His strong, warm hands gently caress my skin as he leans in close. I can smell the faint scent of the other men still lingering on me, and it sends a shiver of excitement through my body.

"You were amazing," he murmurs, his lips brushing against my neck. "So beautiful, taking them all like that." His fingers glide slowly down my arms, tracing patterns on my flesh. "I love watching you come undone, seeing and hearing your pleasure."

I sigh contentedly, melting into his touch. "I love you," I whisper, my eyes fluttering closed.

His hand drifts lower, caressing the sticky wetness between my thighs. I gasp at the sensation, my hips arching up to meet his exploring fingers. "That's it, my love," he croons. "Let me take care of you."

He rubs the mixture of Matt's cum and my wetness into my skin, as if he's fascinated with me being full of another guy's cum.

"You're so incredible," Ian murmurs, his voice thick with emotion. "I'm the luckiest man alive."

I want to tell him that I'm the luckiest woman in the world to have a husband as thoughtful as him, but he kisses me before I can. I sigh from the pleasure as he caresses every inch of my body. His touch is reverent, worshipping every curve. I feel utterly cherished.

Ian's fingers brush circles around my clit, and I shiver from delight. He knows my body so intimately, every sensitive spot that drives me wild. As he strokes me, I can feel the familiar coil of pleasure building deep within me again. Holy fuck, how can I have another orgasm in me?

"That's it," he murmurs, his voice thick with desire. "Just let go."

His thumb presses down on my clit, and I cry out as the delicious waves of another climax wash over me.

Ian holds me close as I tremble in his arms. His eyes shine with raw emotion. "I love you so much. You're my everything."

My heart overflows with the depth of my love for this incredible man as he kisses me softly and settles over me.

His muscular frame presses against me, and I can feel the heat of his body as he slides his cock between my sensitive folds. He moves slowly, letting me feel every inch of him as he fills me completely.

A shudder of pleasure ripples through me, and I gasp at the exquisite sensation. Ian's eyes lock onto mine, his gaze smoldering with barely contained desire. "You feel so good," he murmurs, his voice low and ragged. "So wet for me."

He begins to thrust, his movements agonizingly slow and deliberate. Each drag of his thick shaft sends electric jolts of pleasure coursing through my body. I moan and arch into him, craving more.

Ian lowers his head, trailing hot, open-mouthed kisses along my neck. His stubble scrapes deliciously against my sensitive skin, making me whimper. I hold onto his shoulders as he picks up the pace. The wet sound of our bodies slapping together fills the air. Every thrust makes me moan with delight.

"That's it, baby," Ian encourages, his voice strained with the effort of maintaining his control. "Come for me. I want to feel you come."

Ian's thrusts become deeper and more powerful, hitting a magical spot inside me that makes me see stars. The tension builds until I'm teetering on the edge and desperate.

"Oh god" I cry out, my voice breaking. "I'm so close, please don't stop!"

He moves one hand down to where we're joined, his fingers finding my swollen clit. The dual sensations of his cock filling me and his skillful touch on my most sensitive spot push me over the edge.

My orgasm crashes through me, waves of bliss pummeling me. He comes with me, and I convulse around his shaft, milking him as he groans and unloads ropes of cum deep inside me. My vision goes white and stars explode behind my eyelids as I ride out the incredible high.

When I finally come down, I collapse bonelessly against the mattress. Ian peppers my face with tender kisses, murmuring words of praise and adoration.

"How many times did I come?" I ask breathlessly, looking up at him with hooded eyes.

Ian chuckles, brushing a damp strand of hair from my forehead. "Honestly, I lost count."

He wraps me in his arms, and we snuggle together, basking in the afterglow. "So, does this mean you still want to share me?" I tease, tracing patterns on his chest.

Ian grins wolfishly. "Absolutely. Though, I think I'll be keeping your gorgeous ass all to myself. I'll only let the others play with it on special occasions."

I laugh and kiss him as a feeling of utter contentment envelops me. I float on a cloud of blissful satisfaction, my body humming with the memory of pleasure.

"That was incredible," I murmur, nuzzling into the warmth of Ian's neck. "I can't believe how lucky I am. To have you, to have this."

Ian presses a kiss to my hair. "I'm the luckiest man, baby."

We lapse into contented silence, basking in the afterglow until I have a thought and almost giggle. Oh god, poor Sasha is never going to believe the night I just had. Yeah, I think I'll keep this experience to myself. I'm the perfect, slutty wife who just took on four cocks and lost count of how many times I came.

Ian kisses my head again, and a rush of love for him makes me smile. In this moment, I feel closer to him than ever before. This is exactly where I want to be—wrapped up in his arms, completely and utterly satisfied.

Best. Life. Ever.

The End

Don't miss the story of Erin being shared with Mack, along with a couple of other bonus stories from the series.

Find it on my website:

https://www.lacey-cross.net/theslutthotwife

ABOUT LACEY CROSS

Lacey Cross is a wife sharing erotica writer with over 100 short stories published since she started in 2021. Her stories emphasize the pleasure found from the wife living her best slut life and embracing the hotwife lifestyle. She explores themes of free use, submissive wives with dominant bulls, BDSM... and oh-so-many men.

Find her books, erotic shorts, and audiobooks on her website: https://lacey-cross.com/

If you like romantic BDSM erotica, check out her April Cross books at: https://books.april-cross.com/